THESE THREADS WHO LEAD TO BRAMBLE

THESE THREADS WHO LEAD TO BRAMBLE

FICTION + ESSAYS

RUSSELL PERSSON

2580 Craig Rd.
Ann Arbor, MI 48103
www.dzancbooks.org

First Edition: February 2025
Cover design by Michael Krantz
Interior design by Michelle Dotter
Author portrait by Ahren Hertel

ISBN: 9781938603228

Printed in the United States of America

10 9 8 7 6 5 4 3 2 1

CONTENTS

For Katie

THE HISTORY OF AMERICAN ROAD TRAVEL

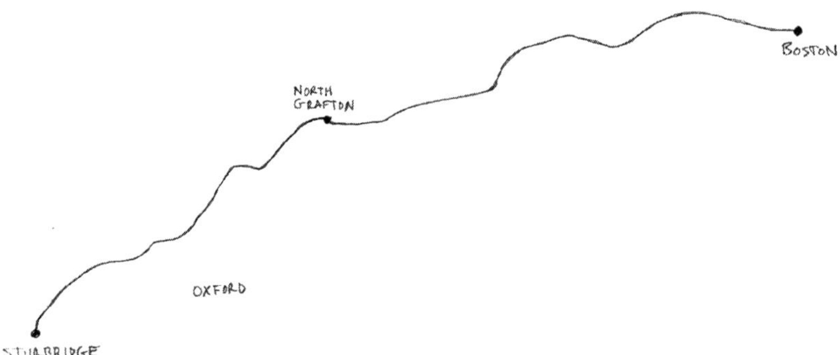
BOSTON
NORTH
GRAFTON
OXFORD
STURBRIDGE

What's recalled returns by chance. Stirred not by some desire to remember but by the taste of mint in the back of your throat or by a slanted light through amber curtains or passing the briefest scent of soap or lotion or by the shape a trail of smoke who rises from a cigarette describes or by the sound a single-engine airplane makes or what's recalled is vivid again by the shift in tone of voice or by the quaver or stirred again by the way a garment hangs or by some unnoticed trip like so many occasions trivial and gone but for a note awaken some bloom who puts together pieces of an older record. There is a name for the history of the lives of saints but there is no name for the sudden chaff we suppose and bear.

~~~~~

The recollection of car rides, of back seats and legs next to legs or where hands go, highways and nights driving, counties and states and regions crossed and re-crossed, the memory a foreign land but wholly familiar, local, a foreign language there but in silence and in brief scenes and storyboards of what we lived, the language falls away and becomes the sounds of an expression, the note who ends the verse.
~~~~~

~~~~~

A college and the city it's in, a loose assemble of friends us all in a car and we drive us all packed to where I grew up an hour west from there. A winter night and wool coats gathered us around the closeness of us all tight quartered in the back seat the steam loading up inside the windows her finger draws letters draws *catapult* into the steam of the back window. How simple is it to recall when this recall has been often, when other pieces of this story remain fled.

The car ride the first night in some communion the love later the beginning of a map. We came together it was nothing it was all. A true abandon and a pulling back and then a true abandon.

Our bones dredge up what seem like years like grand movements of the chorus but are only weeks or months at best. At most or when recalled become markers outside the grid of our olden clocks and journals.

Our bodies loaded close into the back seat driving west to where I grew up to where I left our bodies close and then unknown. What chance was it that it was us there? What alignment arranged that? This all gets us nowhere.

I trust the motion of the planet the loops we mindless make around the sun the stars in night the pinpricks in the sheet above us.

~~~~~

She was from a north land where lakes went uncounted and she lived near a city spread out on that cold plain. The shape of where she was from bewildered me and I could only see one street corner and one backyard where her father honed his green grass.

In college in the spring we had just our devices left to us a week off from school and school shut down to what became a quiet week. We found ourselves bewitched she and I bewitched unlike what else we had known until then. Unable to part and about each other like breathing. The foreground and the background at once. This underwater sense, quiet and complete and surrounded on all sides, this room not safe in full but most alive and vibrant. A week away from her was unjust.

She flew back to the plains and I rode with her on the train to the airport and we walked to the gate. From here I don't recall our severance but instead what's clear is when I rode the train back to the city where we went to school and all sound scuttled to what became light and colors and a cotton stillness came around me on the train the train who went inside the ground and then back out into the sunlight. I got off the train and through some thick pond who now lived around me I went slowly and with no sound only notes muffled by this us we found I went to the curb and stood there in the sunlight. I soaked in what I could. I soaked in what the silence told me, how the new quiet of this big city was constructed of a union urgent by the rules of better chance. The sun was there and laid itself down on me standing at a loss inside the stillness at a loss inside the loss I knew I'd signed. The tearing away in truth what was then a gathering. Sun and stillness and the loss of what then was of course undefined. She flew back to the plains and I stood sunned and quiet with some new chart to go on with no chart in hand.

I walked a few blocks and I crawled through the back window of a friend's apartment and put my head down on his pillow. He'd also flown away for the week and I had nowhere to go. The school was closed and our city was vacant. With my head on his pillow I could hear the sound our city made but it was outside and distant and a small band of sunlight came through the curtains and fell across my shirt. When I closed my eyes she was there and her dark eyes and I could feel her black hair hanging down the sides of me in a room our faces were and her black hair the walls who kept us there. The city sounds near mute and a warm patch on my shirt where the sunlight landed and the city how it continued, continued on.

~~~~~

There was a photograph taken of us but I've never seen it. She was standing up inside an old sedan and I was on the street up against this car. She was standing with herself up out of the sunroof and our foreheads touched because there was no world no time enough to contain the grand shifting of our hearts as we held them there.

He came to us, a photographer from a local paper, and gave me his card and told us what section of the paper we'd be in. Human Interest.

I looked in issues for weeks and never saw the shot but from where I keep these things inside my bones I see it from where it was taken.

~~~~~

What I did have was a photograph of her at a diner. She sits with her back to the counter on a diner stool her elbows back behind her up on the counter top. A white t-shirt and cardigan and jeans and what was not a smile but a warm warning a wager a calling off of all what's not essential an invitation a summons to rise in kind.

THE ENGLISH BAND FELT RELEASED ten albums in ten years. Their fifth album was titled *Let the Snakes Crinkle Their Heads to Death*. The album contains ten instrumental tracks, all brief and all evocative of a certain place or mood. When the album first came out I transferred the album onto a cassette tape and I listened to this tape in my car for months straight. When the album was reissued over thirty years later the title was changed to *The Seventeenth Century*.

The Seventeenth Century

We drove from Boston to Cape Cod in the winter. We drove south and the sky was winter gray and there were piles of snow along the sides of the road and piles of snow in the middle land of the old highway. There is a tall old two-lane steel bridge who crosses a canal and after the bridge is Cape Cod.

The Nazca Plain

Of this trip with her I remember so little and what remains is ill-drawn and silent. The hotel room in Eastham. The light in the hotel room, a Sheraton near the sea the curtains drawn in day and gray light coming into the room around the edges of the curtain a bed as wide as it was long and later in the day and into the night the only light in the room from the bathroom the door mostly shut the sink light on there

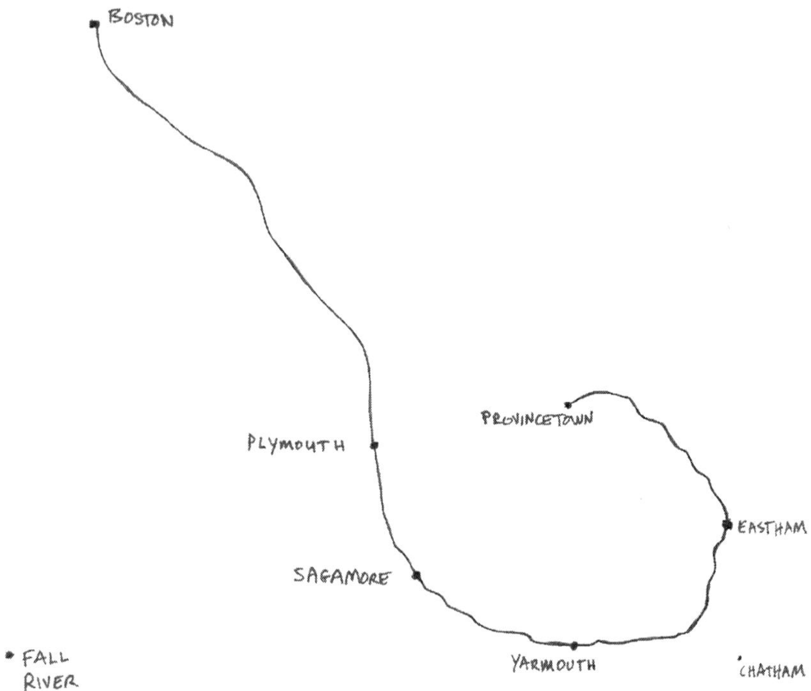
BOSTON
PROVINCETOWN
PLYMOUTH
EASTHAM
SAGAMORE
FALL
RIVER
YARMOUTH
CHATHAM

must be some of this someone else could help fill in but now this is all I can gather.

Ancient City Where I Lived

Her eyes and shoulders her black hair her closing eyes and arms in her slow landing on me the bathroom sink light what of it made its way to us was on her neck and where her neck ran up behind her ear and down the slow bend to her shoulder where her black hair it fell like hair inside a river.

Indian Scriptures

Shouldn't melancholy have the better memory? To forever recross those grounds to always open and lay out what's better left.

The Palace

The way the light slanted into the room from the bathroom door left open a finger or two to let in the light from the sink light this light when after our eyes had learned to see by it was enough in that room a hotel room in Eastham a Sheraton I could not afford we closed the heavy curtains made up of more than one layer of cloth these curtains kept it dark for us all day I can't remember if we ate at all or left to walk or what else we might have done except remain there in that dark except the light who slanted in from the door unshut enough to let in what piece of it lights this of it to me now.

Viking Dress

The way all hotel rooms are alike. The bathroom and an alcove for bags near the entrance, where to hang things on hangers. A low bureau and on top of that a television. A chair no one sits on. Thick curtains and bedspreads made of some unreal fabric. Some lights and a nightstand with a book in it. There must have been our clothes on the floor. Our things in the bathroom. My keys on the low bureau.

- MOUNT SHASTA
- CASTELLA
- REDDING
- CORNING
- WINTERS
- SAN FRANCISCO

OUR ONE SILENT DRIVE an intentional unease. South from Shasta back to our apartment in San Francisco. Five hours. Seven. I watched from the passenger seat the countryside the orchards the hills the passing land and lives and I placed myself inside the landscapes of a different life, whichever life another than the one I lived. In silence builded of a broken day, a broken week. My leaving by now practiced and announced only to myself. My leaving in the works the orchard where I run a test in our silent drive by. Due South in silence. Wrapped in this unease. My voice walled and absent. Why sully what was left of us?

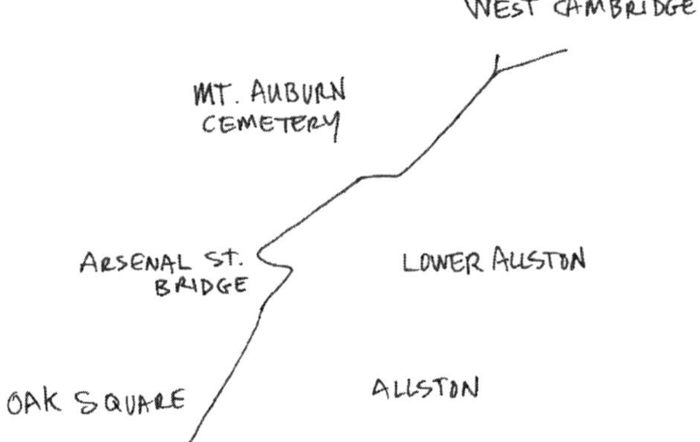
WEST CAMBRIDGE
MT. AUBURN CEMETERY
ARSENAL ST. BRIDGE
LOWER ALLSTON
OAK SQUARE
ALLSTON

FOLLOW A GESTURE FOLLOW YOUR HEART or follow another's eyes follow her eyes and glance from upstairs a gathering inside a house a crowd the music on from upstairs we followed what was unsaid we followed the other downstairs and outside and into the close August evening.

From her slow tidal measure the movements against the pace of what was said the slowness in a gauze around us from this slowness to the August outside our bicycles locked to several trees. From near Oak Square we began on roads with our two bicycles on roads in night or almost morning so the roads were still and empty, she went ahead and I followed and I worked hard to keep up. Through traffic signals and down unlit one-way streets the other way and then left to cut us over the Charles River on the Arsenal Street Bridge. The Charles River in night with its own slowness its own unmeasured floor under darkness under the black pane who bends through Allston. Across the bridge and right I follow her and try to match her pace she's up standing on her pedals pulling away up Coolidge Avenue and to see her was at once a defeat but also when I saw her she was shining and she was a kind of star there up ahead a wonder and leaving me behind. Past the streetlights who cast a green metal light down along Mt. Auburn Cemetery that long stretch of iron gate and fence to keep what all's inside inside. Then into where the houses stood side by each she slowed to cut left and right and led us to the back alley behind her address where we put our bicycles in the garage.

It was late or almost morning. She rented a bedroom in the house of a university professor. We crept through this old fine house and up the stairs and she brought me to her room and in.

Weeks later she wrote me a letter and delivered it by hand to my apartment. She passed the letter through the mail slot and it fell onto the floor inside the door. The message that she left like a seed who stays unplanted and dry; her message remained there but it remained. Years passed before I understood what it might have been like to write such a letter and then I saw her clearly there, walking up the steps to my apartment and kneeling down to open the mail slot and with her right hand pushing through the slot her envelope onto the floor and from there I could begin to trace back her path to where she held a pen and back to how her heart was rent and back again and back to when silent we crept upstairs to her one room.

Some nights we drove until dawn. If we both flagged we'd stop and sleep with the extra shirts we had covering our faces for the shade that was below the shirt and cars would pull in next to us and doors opened and then closed and in a few minutes the car doors would open again and close and the car engine started and in the early sun we heard the cars pull out and drive away and then there was no sound except for the gray murmur of the highway behind us. We slept into the dreams our chaff came up with, loose ambles hard to fathom—in our exhaust we began our dreams quickly so as to all fit them in. Our shirts the shades who kept the days of our accord. How we choose to set the margins against the regular rising of the sun and the setting of the sun.

We will grow old and get sick and then we die but for now we sleep off highways after driving through the night and when our bodies rest our bodies deeply rest and time passes in the shade of what we wear.

~~~~~

The smell of Oklahoma from the back seat where I slept. Half slept and watched you drive when I woke. The moments when I watch you when you're unaware are like the moments when I watch you when you sleep and it's then we both inhabit the stillness born inside us for this one verse. Your nose and jaw and the way your mouth is lit by the
~~~~~

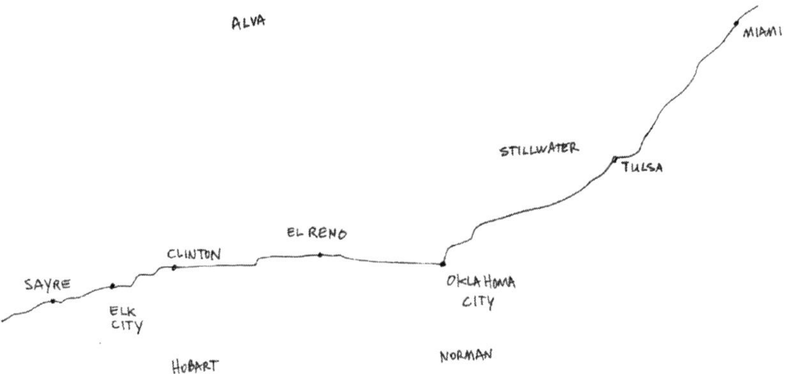
ALVA
MIAMI
STILLWATER
TULSA
EL RENO
CLINTON
SAYRE
OKLAHOMA CITY
ELK CITY
HOBART
NORMAN

lights of cars oncoming and the smell of Oklahoma is shit and fertilizer or some chemical I can't name but has the smell of sharp water and the smell walks back into the walls of my throat and remains there in the night. Your dark hair in night lit up along an ear by the dash lights and I fall again asleep I pull a jacket or shirt over me to cover my eyes and I become asleep again behind you. The gaps in the concrete highway knock a rhythm and this becomes a train to me and the highway sound is the sound of this train on tracks and then I'm inside a dream and this dream describes what death is like.

~~~~~

When we stop at night we listen to the bug sounds. We stand outside and you look out over the field behind the parking lot. Your jeans and your t-shirt are good for long travel. I've seen you undo the button of your jeans and work the waist down over your slight girl hips and down your summer legs with the soft down on them—the down I'll note from then on as something perfect and inviolate—an index of the path my early heart would follow. At night we remain unspoken so instead we listen to the bug sounds different than the bug sounds in New England and I see you leaning with your jeans against the car leaning with a tilted hip a slant I also note and keep with me for long.

~~~~~

We stopped for bottle rockets after passing through St. Louis, somewhere in wooded Missouri.

In early evening the wooded gullies of Missouri gave way to the shapes and flats of what we'd come to know as something Western. With Kansas up above us we crossed into Oklahoma and we drove. The land itself the marker for where we arrived and where we'd left. I learned how state lines are decided not so much by rivers or old clan borders but are instead decided by the color and the shape and the texture of the land. How Missouri changes from Missouri into Oklahoma in the palette and the topography and the geology as New Mexico is the etched basin below the elevated floor of the Texas panhandle.

I slept back-seated and built into my dream was the rhythm of the gaps in the concrete highway and how our tires bumped over them.

We woke up on the top floor of a parking garage in Oklahoma City. There was no roof and so we woke us elevated and above and also exposed. The views for stretches we hadn't known. Some odd color to the sunrise and a hum below and that was the city itself.

You slept the night in the front seat and in the morning when the sun was new you got out of the car and leaned against the concrete wall who ran along the outside of the parking garage. You must have driven us here last night when I was sleeping. To the top floor of a public parking garage. You limber in your jeans and t-shirt and from the back seat I see you there unaware that I'm awake. Your silhouette against the wholly western foreign dawn—you stretched into your utter tallest self and there I set into my unfaded banks the images the frames who remain. How can something unintentional last until we die? What then is unremarkable?

You limber and even then you're a thinner version at your tallest you are nowhere near tall. When I think of you in Oklahoma City in the dawn and stretching tall as tall as you were able there is something within me burning with a brightness I'm unable to measure or describe this felt enormity but also I could stash it all away from view and there sequester it—but we gather here to hear only what we tell ourselves.

~~~~~

I've slept in the back seat of a car heading north from Tennessee. I've slept in the back seat heading west in Oklahoma and I've slept in the back seat heading south through Georgia. I once slept in the back seat of a station wagon driving down a mountain pass from Kennedy
~~~~~

Meadows and then south to Los Angeles. I've slept in the back seat of my own car while someone else drove and I've slept in the back seats of the cars of others and I've slept through long night stretches of desolate highway that smelled of dirt and crops in those moments between sleep when I woke and heard the wheels and the rhythm of the wheels on the highway joints and looked up to see her dark hair and the lights run across her nose and cheek and ear and I've slept in the sun in the back seat in Oakland drunk on afternoon gin and tossing hours away I'd wish back. The back seat as a carrel in between moments. In transition but at the mercy of others.

~~~~~

We must have made our way into the downtown. I didn't have money for a Stetson but we agreed we'd find a Western-wear store downtown and at least go inside.

~~~~~

Single words of what was said. But like music the half-notes fall away and what remains is the tone, the cadence, the shift of any eyebrow, the quaver in a morning reminder when a heart was new wounded and the cut stood bright. Single words. If any. This mosaic assembled and often false, just a near version of what was.

All the eyes who had the same expression you had. All of every set of eyes who entered into that vast unknowing that unattached and had no wrangle no moor no good root no where to start. The next eyes who would ask as yours had asked.

It turns out we're graded not by what we contain but instead by our elisions.

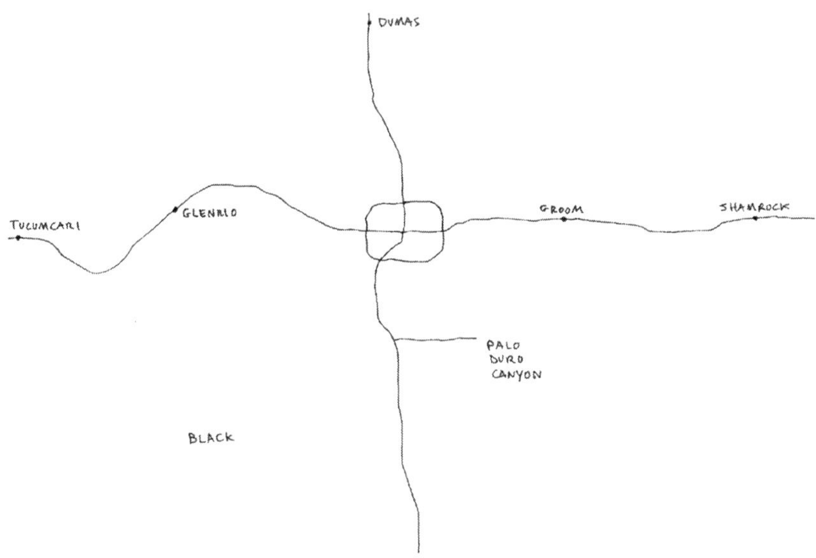
DUMAS
TUCUMCARI
GLENRIO
GROOM
SHAMROCK
PALO
DURO
CANYON
BLACK

Texas. An afternoon panhandle, then Palo Duro Canyon and the horses there. We rented horses for an afternoon but what of all this remains is not so much the horse and she was good and brown and went herself as slowly but what remains is not only you and your smile looking back at me from your brown horse but instead the terrain and rocks and the shadows and the contours of the canyon and the dry wash where silt was sculpted into a smooth trough and the deep horse muscles who walked slowly so I could ride and see all this but also our cloudless afternoon I don't believe it rained once that drive we took west I don't believe it rained once that month that summer there was not a day of rain one day that year we drove us for the first time west.

Does it make a difference if I say it was a bright morning in that downtown, or if it was a cloudless day in Palo Duro Canyon?

~~~~~

We kept on west. From Palo Duro Canyon we must have headed back up toward Amarillo and the beltway there. To Interstate 40 West and the service road who runs alongside the highway for miles.

Driving from Texas into New Mexico I saw for the first time the land fall away. As if the state line was a decision of topography or geology. From Texas the highway descends into New Mexico and it's
~~~~~

clear the tops of the buttes are at the same elevation as the plateau of the Texas panhandle and what you descend into is the land washed away by some ancient flooding we're unable to imagine in terms of years and rivers and the silt they move between. The eroded land is red muscle underneath the skin of the West.

In Tucumcari we stayed at the Palomino Motel, the cheapest on the strip. Old Route 66 and the excellent neon. This was decades ago and there were still unaltered remains of the old U.S. highway. Unique motels and diner food and drug stores named after the families who owned them for decades.

Tucumcari. It must have been late afternoon. Your olive skin would have been at its most arresting in the light when the sun has gone down but there is still the red and orange glow in the sky and there are no shadows and the wind has died down and it is not yet as cold as it will get tonight and all the colors of you and where you are and what's behind you near you are all at their most vivid and alive the colors are the skeleton of these brief moments called up in memory and sustained there.

THE HISTORY OF SEVERAL EUROPEAN COMPOSERS

ALBAN BERG

LYRIC SUITE

1.

In the first movement of Alban Berg's Lyric Suite (Allegretto gioviale), Alban learns the bones who run inside him the bones who sung together make up inside him the tallness he was given these bones who the next day have holed up inside him in the coral mud of them it is Alban learns his bones would change. He first learned his bones were inside him. Then Alban learns his bones would change and this is in night. He is in bed in night and it is warm up on the second floor even with the shutters open and there are bug sounds in odd cadence outside and he is in bed in the notice of the pain his creaking stretching bones make inside him.

In night inside him where his sounds began their courses into music where from in his bones the bars would come and him along the bars go dotted in the notes who came from in him he knew his bones were like the armature of a maquette but he didn't know his bones would change.

If his bones, he imagines in night his racing night, fell into the floor of his bag down in the shins and inside his ocean feet, the click of all this would be like the three notes of the bug outside who beats three times and in the final notes of this first movement those bugs who run in threes collect the sound of fallen bones they come apart and drum down to the bag the floor.

2.

The second movement of Alban Berg's Lyric Suite (Andante amoroso) begins at the Berghof near the Ossiarcharsee in Carinthia. Upstairs Alban lies in bed and in the summer it is warm upstairs and so his bedroom windows are open the shutters folded into the room and collapsed against the window frames and from outside his open windows are the crickets and the sounds of crickets and the small sick birds who carry the crickets off through the weeds and the tall grass and there is also the sound of the wind and what the wind becomes inside the leaves outside his window what the leaves become with the wind inside them and all this along with the hum inside Alban this hum which is his excess his engine who cannot stop or settle in night his excess his seventeen years come to this in night him unslept and lively. The zest and unsettle his bones are a part of him and this all builded in his bones and from there spoken as one who hums is never alone for the always of it. Spoken like a color of light and ember.

Downstairs on the floors below him only the ones who serve inside the Berghof are still about arranging things back to where and he is awake for no certain cause other than his own excess who still runs about inside him with a blue and grown avast who needles out from inside him and sets him up awake in night.

3.

In the third movement of Alban Berg's Lyric Suite (Allegro misterioso—Trio estatico) she comes to him and he is uncontained and in his excess. He is already rigid and he thinks ahead to when she turns the handle of the door with an evening hand. She comes to him and with her she will bring herself and how she enters and he is uncontained.

In night she comes to him a quiet hand to let her in and she closes the quiet door behind her. She has with her a pitcher of water and the candle she blows out and sets the sterling candlestick on top of his wooden dresser. She crosses the room the wool rug and sets the pitcher on his bedside table. He can smell her now and she smells of what she washed after the dinner and of the paraffin and lemon she rubs into the dining room table after the plates have been cleared when she's alone to clean.

She takes a corner of his bedsheet and pulls it off from him and he is rigid and a chill runs through him even for the summer night and it's warm still in his room but his uncontain sets a coldness in him and he tries to master himself against the shiver who comes. Get up and stand over there is what her open hand says to him. With Alban standed now and his rigid standed out from him he watches her remove her apron and sit down on the bed. Her eyes come up to meet his and she keeps her eyes remained on his and removes her shoes and stockings and stands to remove her skirts who fall down to the wool rug and she removes what is underneath her skirts her eyes remain on his and what is underneath her skirts falls now to the wool rug and to the floor. Turning her back to him and lifting her hair it is then Alban sheds the rug the yard between them and unfastens what has her dressed yet to fall it to the floor. The moon lends its tin light down on Marie as she sits back down on the bed and lays herself back her eyes remain she sets herself into the middle of his narrow bed. The moon itself is trusted and she fixes him down to her so that the same moon is on them both at once a window open and she contains him down to where and she contains him in her steady school.

The final notes are something of a dwindle, the music of it unmoored and underway and becoming more distant and less defined as a face becomes a different face in the almost true dark and there is only the smallest angle of light up along the visage and it turns from one into another and it's only guessed what mood is carried and before the shape is well sussed a scattering comes and the low almost inaudible notes blow off the bow to die off on each a several and small path.

4.

It is described in the fourth movement of Alban Berg's Lyric Suite (Adagio appassionato) that the Berg family calls her Mizzi, an informal play on Marie. Mizzi goes to Alban's room in night to fuck him to not so much speak with him but to be with him and she lends her past to these evenings and he begins to learn her maps and wake. She lends the olden shapes of what has come about her over her the bodies she has known they've come to her before, before Alban. The hard men who rushed and the quiet one who arrived on himself and there was one who was amused it remains on her like the borders and lines who draw the story of a hillside. In Alban Mizzi finds a dear study an upstairs boy the young Alban with his fuck out racing ahead of him and shy of any measure. She wants to fold him twice, like a sheet, when a sheet is new and unpressed. Then unfolded and gathered in her own fuck.

5.

In the fifth movement of Alban Berg's Lyric Suite (Presto delirando—Tenebroso) we come to find Alban who walks a path by the Ossiarcharsee in Carinthia with himself along a path who is enough in width for just himself and worn down to the dirt by others who walk here in the shaded wooded stretch and later where the path goes closer to the water and the edge of land against the lake. On clouded days and when the wind is at its least down at the water he can see into the depths where at a slant even then the deepness goes beyond his seeing and what continues under there beyond his seeing is beyond all knowing and contains there a possible key to what all else is unlit. These near vessels of what's dark we can just walk down to along the path who leads him from the Berghof to the Ossiarcharsee.

He constructs a quick obituary. After failing school young Alban sunk himself below a lake in summer. His shoes were found by the shore and a search for a farewell letter turned up only a few leaves.

By the lake there is no one in wait and nothing or no one to wait for and so when he is stray as such from the lines who lead him back to them he becomes stray himself and settles into where there is no watch or any question. Loosed upon nothing he hears the wind and across the lake when it is still a voice carries over from the far side and then a bird.

His mother at the Berghof in her own new stillness.

It is said our elders see to themselves as they've seen to us.

6.

In the sixth and final movement of Alban Berg's Lyric Suite (Largo desolato) Alban is thirty-nine and a respected composer living in the Hietzing district of Vienna with his wife Helene and their housekeeper Anny Lenz. There is an afternoon in Hietzing when Helene is away on a cure and a young woman arrives unannounced to the Berg residence to request permission to take a photograph of the composer. Alban invites the young woman inside. A portrait on the street is unbecoming and indoors a better setting can be arranged. Inside, the young woman reveals herself to be Albine, the daughter of Alban and Marie Scheuchl, Mizzi.

"Because of her beautiful bone structure, she sat for Hans Domenig's 'Muttergottesstatue', a Madonna and child sculpture."

—Pat Bamford-Milroy, Grete Kocher

In the final bars of the sixth movement, Alban Berg, fifty years old, having just written a violin concerto in memory of and dedicated to Manon Gropius, forever skeptical of doctors and obsessed since youth by the number twenty-three, is bitten by a winged insect and does not have the infection treated and a few weeks later Alban dies, in the final notes of the Lyric Suite, on December 24, 1935.

Largo desolato, in musical notation, implies a slow, grand, but solitary phrase.

ERIK SATIE

THREE PEAR-SHAPED PIECES

First

I'VE NAMED ALL MY NAME-DROPPING FOR THE NIGHT and by Christ it's time for me to walk although another treat of cognac might help us all along.

There is no good sir. No welcome to the evening of the evening. But there my patrons the gentlemen the ladies they go and file out themselves back to their own good homes. A brief gentle walk home. But us here I say there is still no good sir. Just lamps out and the rest going out. Tamped.

Headed home I go and stumble south. The wooden handle of my hammer where it meets the metal head is worn smooth from where I hold it there inside my coat inside my pocket and believe me I'm at the ready do believe me. Fucking scoundrels in the shrubs or hiding in the corners. Would as much to be the tack hammer your noggin wants. Headed south and from the Auberge it's mostly downhill until we get us to the Seine. Cocked on evening whisky then it comes to me I've lived a certain life. Wouldn't want this recall to run amiss and so let's take it down. So take this message. I regulate my life.

This is what I do and when: I rise in early morning. Three hours and five minutes after I become inspired and this goes on for one hour and twenty four minutes. And then I take a lunch. An excellent lunch who takes up no longer than four minutes of my day. For quite soon after I become on horseback to survey the grounds I've come to collect by now. I sweep an arm if you can notice me from where you are. Then this horse I'm off and back to being burdened by the muse who doesn't let me ride. I come indoors to become profound inspired.

In the evening at 7:16 I sit to dinner served. Four minutes after is when I'm done with dinner and then I spend over one full hour on God knows what until we begin the night of symphonic readings out loud. Make of this what you will as of what you've made til now. For then I'm off to bed at the strike of 10:37 night. I sleep soundly unless the day is Tuesday which is when I awake with a start at 3:14 morning and again of this you can what of it would you will.

My food is white as in the whites of eggs and the inside of bread, coconuts, rice, the fat of dead animals, sugar, cotton salad, salt, turnips, shredded bones and certain fish who've been skinned.

When I breathe I breathe distinctly out with pleasure and when I walk I walk with my hands upon my ribs and I see well behind me and crane accordingly to the aft. I wouldn't tell you how I sleep for it would be a true confound. But do let it be known my one eye remains open while the other rests, and so on. And my bed—I'll save you all the time and not go further into what describes such an odd contraption no one would believe in either way but suffice it to say if it'll do to tell let's say a cavity has been cut who saves a room for my dear noggin thank you and good night.

Continue us to walk continue me to walk in due south absolutely.

The Pont Neuf an option this evening.

Though Jesus Christ what with all my cognac I might just with Saint Denis lug my head the halfway home tonight to choose where I might rest this awful melon.

With my hands upon my ribs I walk and here and there reach into where in my pocket our night hammer sits. I worry some the handle where it meets the metal head where I lay upon the patina one more thin coat of hand oil or soot from where I've been it is the dust we pick up in the day when we're looking elsewhere.

My stumble my amount I walk me home. The different routes and then the same ones and ones who wouldn't tell the way I wend.

The farther from Montmarte I get. The farther from the Seine and from the Pont Neuf and again we come us up from that black river to the south and what comes with this. In night in time the smell of boiling cows and hides who must in their aroma set out to tell us this is no way to skin a cat. But home it is and I welcome me back to the slum I've kept and kept well hidden from them all.

Second

Well it was like he never thought it through, said the man who moves pianos to his wife. I've not seen a thing like it. Not in all the days I've been.

Soup? said the wife of the man who moves pianos to the man who moves pianos.

The second christing floor, up two flights. We had her legs off this grand of course. No other way to get it up. And him all suited to the nines and dapper bringing up the legs like a boy carrying cord wood I swear, said the man who moves pianos to his wife.

The nut with the pince-nez? I thought he already had a grand up there, said the wife to the man who moves pianos.

Well I tell you he does. The first one we moved up there. It must have been years ago when we lugged that first one up. And then I thought well he must have gotten rid of the first one, but wouldn't I know of a goddamn piano moved in Arcueil? Did he pull it apart and heave it out the window into the street I'm asking? The absolute shit of it all is that his first piano, the one I moved it must have been years ago, is still in his second floor room, right where we left it the first time. Nearly shat my britches. Right where we left it. So Alex, he'd gone ahead to scout the room and comes back down and says there's already a grand in his one room and there's no place else for another. So I go up to his room and he's there and would you believe me if I told you on top of his head was a piece of fabric, a napkin, black, draped over his head like some kind of veil and he's still as a board and he must have heard me standing there and he says, Good sir, I wear this for your protection, so I won't know you've been in my house, and for mine, for I don't prefer the sun. Now Alex, he never said a thing about a black napkin but you think he might have mentioned that little nugget so I stand there and I ask him where we're supposed to put this loving piano we've got now half up his steps and he, get this, he lifts up just a corner of his napkin to see for himself and he points to where his piano is already and says, There. He says, There, just put it on top of this one—I've already cleaned it off for you and so there you go—just put it there.

You see, dear. Not only is he a piece of work, said the wife to the man who moves pianos, but so might you be a piece of work as well.

Third

A Way of Beginning

What I would like to do this evening is arrange my white collars in their good order of stiffness, from stiff to not, along the outside edge of my top cabinet—and curl this arrangement around if I must.

More of the Same

I don't hear a soul in the hall so I can now go out to the Parc d'Ecole d'Arcueil. We will need some water for this evening and it is there we'll find an excellent draught. We'll bring two bottles and a bag.

Piece I

When I'm arranged or near arranged what calls me away is one lone mosquito, possibly desperate but more likely languid and hopeful, sent here I am sure of it by Freemasons who have no objectives of their own but to flounder the plans of others. I'll find you dear buzzing bug. You can not be just a sound forever.

Piece II

He wants in, sometimes, that Claude. As if he's uncommon. Though in what way is he not? Do we not all answer to the same muse? Whose his is mine, mine is his. Ungovernable and hidden only by what portion of the moon we choose to see.

Piece III

A banana becomes white when the pants are off. Almost I could say this goes for some other hobbies. Habits. I wrest the time to become in brief inspired. Oh, the notes come and some go and they come in dull flourish and they come full whittled to the bare unadorned without-pants amount of message I've been on the lookout on.

What's More

I could have ended even earlier but I say the resolution hangs in air like the best gnat or noseeum. We go about this calmly.

Rehash

My slow waltz with you my dear my dear self. Me, the sea-bird's nephew. The one who walks slowly with an air of attention, amusement and curiosity and at times inside it's anything other. What stars might gather in their nosey gaze upon my walk I walk me home.

ANTON WEBERN
BAGATELLES AND MOUNT OLIVE

On the composer Anton Webern and the soldier Raymond Norwood Bell

Mittersill

So as not to muck the rest and dream of his grandchildren he went to the front stoop to use his cigar outside and stood there in night, the new quiet still unsure to settle, low dust in eddies few streetlamps who put tents of light down. He listened to the night sounds, the bugs and whine the fucking called to in serial peeps and ticks. The ticks a period among the longer peeps drawn out as a sentence in fond repeat. Could we get by with just a sound and none other? His smoke goes up and off and thins into what could be silence. We thin us like this and to our kin we gather what we can and set it there for them to be with it to be with us as an ashen gray figure drawn on linen I could have it either way I could note and in so doing my notes go ahead of me as a new present. Each night is a new bafflement I strain to harbor any sense of it so the unorder of a distant engine is the undernote to the tin pot hit up against an evening sink. This is him in night his smoke guylined to the weather he's under.

From in his house a voice who comes up into a loudness and heavy bootsteps come from the kitchen and arrive to him through the parlor and as the bootsteps near him a child on the top floor begins a jag and nearer now the bootsteps come to the front door where he holds his cigar away from him and exhales another evening cloud who thins and but for the chaotic winds even low as they are tonight they sow his cloud into a spreaded banner frayed into a gone threadedness and in its dissolve an added note for what maps it ends up on, melded into the endless and next, his glowed tobacco held now in front of him as if his hand was in a greeting to the night and behind him the coming bootsteps and then it is an open door his own door swung in so that a latch undone is a pluck to enact the drawn tones of a dry hinge, an opening as a whip begins the high ringing who follows it and coming through the opened door with his boots and with his widened eyes and with his olive drab and patches who rank him and put his name upon himself and in his hand which is also held out in front of him as if in a greeting is a sidearm. The soldier comes outside in such a rush he comes into the ember of the cigar who swung around to see him and lit edges of it fall down and taking the man outside for a sudden threat he tightens his sidearm hand and conducts the final few notes of the man who was outside now rubbed out in night the tether now cut for good who ran down to him from above.

Mittersill

An olive egg. An early enlist.

He'd gone into the service as a cook a lark his sergeant signed him in for. But any break in the formal he'd become unguided and so it was on the stoop in night an ember toward him was an unknown and he became a sudden shot.

Debriefed the cook was told he ended what was then the life of one composer the peers of whom were few and well upheld.

The cook then gathered in. His body smallened by the sadness who builded in him. He wept in long stretches in Mittersill and wrapped his arms around himself in a try to push his small self back to when he hadn't yet put his kill in. Back into the young bag he wraps him up to go beyond a mourning he's unaware of until it deepens again and then again again.

Mittersill

He's found out who he's offed. He's akin to what he's done. The cook in olive drab has shut the life of one man in night a man who put down these scores in compose, a man who went and wrote his music so that his notes could in their own antic way convince an ear of how true the notes were. This is what's the world, and so to hear it. The cook in olive drab he's balled up he comes to try to shut himself of what he's done.

An army cook his name is Raymond Bell. His sentence is his own handed down. A stone monastery has become a ward for the unable and the shocked. He's decided what he's done is so beyond the criminal that so rent he'll keep on without hinge and without feck. He's cotted inside the unruined end of the monastery. He's cotted there with other broken men and to the limestone wall he's any man. But to himself up to the wall he's in compare a death man who deals in end days who rides the shoulders of well men into the war fields and aliates his death cards to whomever.

I tell you of the days unlived you were verged on. I do come to cancel the coming days you believed you had. And as a seer is taken over by the body who speaks through him so you would commit this sound to sheets the paper staffed and soon endotted with your ear's trance upon them. I am the taker of those days and I am the one who blots out for good all that.

And balled up he'll be carted soon to a stone room away from the rest of them. He'll lean himself in rocking and to mutter how he's a dark agent of all men and how his initial opus is an elegy.

Sea

Shipped home for his fondness there was only room in the ship's brig for him and so locked up was underway his belted coat who kept his arms in. There was no food this cook would allow in him and in his best dwindle when it seemed there could be no end to the crossing of the sea and there was no weather or sky to split up the days into steps but only when the brig officer turned out his desk lamp in night was it night. The dwindle of his arm and of what sense was still left of him when a shift went across him inside and he could tell the legs of this ship were in cold dangle and each leg became ice and broke off below and left him to not know what aim was had at all but to drift and to try to picture for himself what no land in sight would be.

Carolina, Mount Olive

His home and his rooms. Where his wife is and his young son. His gaze does not lift up above her shoulders. His coming home is gathered small, some others he'd known before he left to go to war. When they leave and he is now home with his child son and with his wife he finds himself among the same chairs and side tables and the same smell and the rug who holds a footprint like beach sand. The quiet and the arms of his wife and the eyes of his son he builded into the safe bay he thought could be the wend out of where he'd kept on.

Outside a cicada went through a slow incline to an almost electric hum and others joined in in this mad bug lunacy. A lunacy he'd known all along and home again it greeted him in the first night and kept him awake against the rest he needed and against the long his wife had gathered. But his awayness was steady and did not ebb although he was now home but his deathing over there was a coat he could not put off. The cicada hums went on into the night in a way he'd known when he was young a way to tell how hot and wet it was outside and how slow a body should become inside the day to not get bothered by the day and it is a cloud inside an ear. The summers return to mind and the good hours before night when a pond was swum or when a road into the town was thumbed and then in summer it was the evening hours when a string who held a light dress on a shoulder was sided away and the untanned eyed you as a line who was forbidden. He lies containing what he's done. He makes a bed of the cicadas and falls into this bed alone among his wife and they swim there as some ponds well about them.

In dawn he is awake and unslept. His awayness. Carried like a loaded sledge is pulled across the rotted floors of wooded land. His awayness as a gift offered back to the giver. In day a quiet gone.

The zinnias have come up. Your mother has been over to help with them. Her green fingers I swear.

His answer is a sketch. An abstract who makes no certain land.

Before it's known to him he's assembled days and his body walks in step to the guide stones laid out there for him to follow. In days he's in a service shop and his son comes with him to watch his father meddle on small engines and motors. His son watches close and the quiet class he's in is what holds fast into the days beyond these. The lock washer and then the bolt. A spring made small by the turning of a screw turned by his father's hand.

Raymond Bell sits himself in dusk. He puts his whiskey in him. And sits outside among an air he's on about. Coming around him an air in night who sheds a day and a field smell of how it's fed and kept alive is abundant and near him the zinnias live in open call to the hues God bestowed on them we all come hued by God. The whiskey in him bends his eyes slanting enough to go unguided across his hand and back. He sits and his soft eyes wander untold to where.

Mount Olive: Mäßig

He went in thick and without wait. A habit picked up over there wherein wine came with dinner and whiskey was brought out to follow. His regret is endless and in his cups it becomes a tangle and louder. The fiction and the true of it gathers in him and he hauls it with him and forth if an ear would have it.

His days are doldrums strung together along a valley floor. In night his drink puts a clearing out for him to roam and then in deeper still he's fallen along with his drink into the room where all his voices are kept and it's there he's found in night to mix with them and fend and to rebut again what they've posed in endless chorus about the ruin he's done and the act he can't undo to fend on all points from all assembled to post about him all cases against. It is pinned on him he's host to the voices pinned and left there for the others. An added drink and he's on point again to ward them and not until the drink's enough to rest him it's then he'll camp where God has chosen for him to camp and it could be outside or it could be on a tile floor in a sideways sitting attitude his wife will find him in tomorrow.

His days are doldrums or in night his drink it lifts him from the act he's weighted under. Casted up off into the lighted rooms he's drunk. His coat is gone and his warm eyes are lifted. His drink has recovered days tonight. God chosen a rest to place him in as well and settled there is where he's found.

Waked he spends an off day learning. The Second Viennese School. Tonal scales. Brief bagatelles who disarm an ear.

He copies out the notes who mean to him what runes might but he's sure to fill in the black ovals and leave the open ones open.

With his son in dusk they sit on the back stoop with crickets. Rubbing two fingers he shows his son the movements of the legs of each cricket and the sound who brings itself from this. One across another to show his son the way this sound is made.

Mount Olive: Leicht bewegt

Tip teetering up his stoop it comes they come with it wrapped and it has a man on each corner and in time they dip down and the whole body of it sways tilting backward and they correct this and steady what they bring into the house and go slowly through the middle of the front door who's held open with a boot this shuffle of them slow and meaty like a men's team trying slow for a spell and almost winning at it but for the grunts they do for a body does what it has always done and so the bag of tricks is endless in its own making so the men come up with gutterals and engine exhales each a corner man who lobbies his angle to the men to see if it'll pass so they shuffle loudly to the hall where on the walls a picture of a new recruit hangs who then was ready to do battle and set to bring his violence into the day he sees himself then as new to war and what a kid he was to the actual script who was in store for him all written in the dark gothic hand of the old world arranger his ignorance a blessing then and coming through the hall now the men decline rest but shuffle on up to the jamb of where they intend and it's shrunken down the width in which they get to pass with this and the shrunken door is eyed for wideness so the men on each corner shift themselves to cause a better thinness among them and they sidle through into the guest room with the school piano who needs to be held in place and set up next to and tuned by a kind of listener who would know the way to tune such odd boxes as this one got for no money and the men lended by a church who looks down upon soldiers with a kindness and they install as far as they know how to install this school piano in a room who wants some room already the leveling of which is beyond them all and so it sits with a wooden shim below the southeast leg and stares him down as much as a thing has ever done yet.

Mount Olive: Ziemlich fließend

The clerk from town hall she also tutors how to play these keys. He ends days with her in his guest room the school piano room. They study scales and how a hand rises to the keys and posture. The dusk it reddens them and he studies and is quick to get down the new lesson and go on to the next.

She leaves and he continues but it's now he brings out his transcriptions and walks along each to note by the next buckwheat note in his room the versions he's copied over. In night he tops himself off with the whiskey he's kept home and as if reading the sounds of a language unknown to him he taps what he sees and it could not be so. There must be more time spent in learning it seems. There must be some shift he's not seeing on how to bring these written notes into a room as they are meant.

He presents his transcriptions to his tutor one evening and she plays them. They are in the air inside the school piano room and with them disbelief. She plays them again to be sure.

Less than a minute some notes who tend to something other than a tune it's up to wonder what at all he's up to if the transcriptions are aligned and true.

You must have had them wrong.

Mount Olive: Sehr langsam

He's sure that he's sure of his notes. Alone he causes them into the room and they have an awkward dance a halting rise and then sudden plucks to tell us what? Is it a knocking an invitation or is it a bird in dusk or just a finger in the passing of an idle when? He causes them again in their written briefnesses. He moves them into the school piano room and in there the notes place themselves around him in a shifting fug they all roam and fidget and cannot wear his trust and so they feint and ebb. At once against the roof and on the floor and they lay a seeing upon him to best govern his hands and weigh his versions.

He's fled into the dark hallway and in the kitchen his wife has left on for him a lamp he needs and his son is sleeping and his wife is. So as not to muck the rest and dream of them he puts no ice in his glass but instead a straight whiskey and small water and to keep his trips to few he doubles and more his cup and swigs there in the kitchen a deep pull. He goes back into his piano room and sits again with his copied notes.

They are there still but now hiding but now waiting for him to enact them back to where they can dance and run him through. He plays on and moves them out again.

He pulls deep on his whiskey and a true exhaust comes over him but there is no one to spell him. He plays on into the morning these odds he's sure of and he's sure he has them down.

But the ending notes don't have the body of an ending. It is the middle of a path who gets cut off. An open door who blows a small wind through. Like an unfinish he's a part of now.

He pulls deep on his whiskey and there it's only the keys who remain and look back to him and they do this in the dawn. There is no way to know his path out of that room and to the low chair he sleeps in. The lamp he no longer needs. The good dreams who could have a say in his forgiveness he's too lit to read well and they go lost to him.

Mount Olive: Außerst langsam

I shot him in a moment when his ember turned and swung up to me in its ember color in the night an ember who it seemed was up against me in a violence who would have done me in we could have been surrounded and the son in law Mattel had posted at the doors a thug each who would handle us if it all went sour and for Mattel it did go that way and on my guard and through his house with my warlong nerves who went frayed from what a man endures in it and with my sidearm ready and with my order to return with more men to bring Mattel to the brig we had set up in what was once a town bank I came to the door and drew it in to go outside and thugs were of a possible so when the dark coat swung around and brought an ember round and to me it was unknown it was as far beyond me as it could have been that he stood there in night to seek quiet and to enter into that place who held for him those deep tricks and where he kept those notes who went ahead of him and led him to that plucking and to the spaces in between the notes who grew into sounds themselves for all the space they builded and to the notes who felt as if they tumbled down the steps and fell out on the path to rise again stumbled off without notice or word to where it was they set off to and just before they went away into the darkness you could tell they faltered in a slant in odd routes so they led him in the place he went who held silence only altered by his own device his own adding to the dance he must have held inside him to the place who sketched him his country in which the entire of it was of his sole direction it was here he must have brought himself to in night when the sounds of the city went away to remain him with the rest of it in a study of how the rest of it fit together and the divine could assemble it but instead he swept it all up for his self to build and men go to the end without a country to them and without a dance at all and swung around to me was just an ember who came around his dark coat and embered there and still as if I could one day unsee this and I still I do and tear this out please tear it out from me the wire glasses and his eyes.

Mount Olive: Fließend

Olive Mountain. Wayne County. Maplewood. Valley, Crest, and Kornegay.

Pete's Spa. Before he closes. A pocket jar to walk with.

Life a borrowed better list.

I'm warm to you my night. It is when I'm warm to you.

Center and Main. To look but it's then forever crickets and the sound they rub to me. Rexall's.

September fifteen. Do celebrate me and what I've done. The jar is up and we Prost! Let's off.

East Main, East John. The flatness of us. Why can't these train tracks just sit and mean the tracks they are? I won't fall into that. They go on and off from here.

Down trees and lanes. The jar a good aid for all this. These come to be my neighbors of all the luck. Slatted boards and shingle I can tell it could be the same inside the newspapers the carpets the scent who remains from an oven on. My own goddamn sidewalk. And this jar on a quick retreat. Figure you would have been around for more tonight. Come to the end of the block down here where it ends.

Maplewood in night is not much. Again just what they are, marble set up on end and names cut into the sides. Dates and a dash. The hollow of that dash there, all what goes between the left date and the next.

So let's dwell on this then. Some jar it was who gave it up so early. Riddance. As an altar to you, too dark to see who you it is.

Bees in bonnets. Bustle. A quick walk back into town. Skirting the wife and son. May darkness become what it must and do it soon. What pub'll set me up tonight. I'll pledge to the town I won't bring it up.

Good Mike. Whiskey and an ale back. I keep it to myself.

And what'll become of what I wander to. She doesn't know about the ones I've hidden in the arbor.

THE HISTORY OF AMERICAN PHOTOGRAPHY FROM 1936 TO 1979

PART 1

Who left us where the living equal the dead?
Avedon lets us choose what of his pairings.

His notes on decay and on the measure of the young.
How one haunts the other forever.

Avedon believed that fathers never die.
This is false and this is also true.

We all what have we done is hauled out and haunted.
Left to drift unannounced and we all have a pond for this.

My grandmother Nana showed me photographs she'd taken, saved in albums arranged by date, the descriptions of each photograph entered in the facing page in a single entry line, a long ink box for that purpose, the descriptions written in her excellent cursive.

Nana's apartment in Oxford was on my way home from high school in Shrewsbury.

I don't remember what we talked about but we would, after a while, sit on her bright green couch looking at photographs from recent holidays, the latest additions to the photo albums, or from older albums arranged by dates before I was born, relatives I'd never known sitting closely on a sofa in Queens, or in their bathing suits at Rockaway.

I found a book of Richard Avedon photographs in the stacks along with other used art books.

Before the photographs is an introduction by the artist and in it he tells us his belief that fathers never die.

We can revisit this.

For now I've turned some pages and gone ahead and at the stacks of a junk store I'm left to notice how Avedon paired his portraits and what of each portrait was the piece of it who haunted him enough. What of the left and what of the portrait on the right.

Fathers in Sicilian catacombs.

Sons of fathers in Louisiana madhomes.

Mad sons who mis-guessed the shape of their own fathers on the floor now in a smock their days a long crawl.

Fathers hung up in robes to dry out underneath Palermo.

Fathers never die and so walk among and along with us. The shade of an often word almost aloud. His terms on how to live. Slept an afternoon the radio on the grass on.

The sum of us is hauled out and haunted. Left to drift unannounced and gone as quick.

Each body buried after all. The vessel in time unfit. Avedon also knew this.

Warhol opposite Dovima. In geography the center is an ilium on her, and him a stitch who once kept his quilted chest together. This ilium a roadsign forward underneath an unlikely bow. Andy Warhol shot and serviced and left to be alive again. His hands the hands of one who works with his hands. Her single toe and heel as if to say this pose, held in brief balance, is all you get and almost over.

We go buried and continue us haunting them. Our lot in life it's them who won't end us.

Hamlet's father was a dead father who also wasn't dead. But sometimes in *Hamlet* it's not clear how to guess the dead from the haunting.

Ophelia's death cannot be staged and so the news of her drowning is delivered by Gertrude, the Queen of Denmark. This announcement by the Queen begins with cartography. The location of a tree near a brook.

Soon the tree is envious, according to the Queen. Or at least a pendant bough of it. A sliver.

There is a painting hangs inside the Tate. It is *Ophelia* by John Everett Millais. She's in the brook, having snapped the willow boughs above it with herself. Her dress is wide and like the water.

Her eyes are open still. Is this the moment, before her logged dress pulls her under, when she sings pieces of old songs? For a moment an otter on her back her gaze unasleep but near ready to give in.

Soon she haunts two men to blows inside her grave.

I have a photograph of a house my father lived in when he was young. In Worcester, on the top of Dead Horse Hill. This could have been when he also had a German dog named Peach. The house is tilted and off center in the photograph and there is nothing in the middle of the frame but a dormer and two windows. The edges of the print are scalloped like many photos were in the 1940s.

I have a photograph of my first dog named Gravy.

I have a photograph of a woman she is near the sea she is shading her eyes from the sun she holds a corner of her mouth in a squint she does her haunting she has the sea behind her.

I'm left to notice a photograph is an open cheat to the pact we have with the impermanent.

Jack Gilbert called it the angel lost in our bodies.
The music that thinking is.

What each of them who face each other have in common among how several they are.
The mad poet Ezra Pound and the near dead father.
The dancer Hugh Laing and opposite him at the end of a row of beds in a southern madhome a thin man is checked by a belt who runs from his bedframe to his wrist.

Where would you be to put your ear up against any of this?
What would the sound be?

I visit a man who believes himself clairvoyant. He has his needles he puts in me and we speak about my past in terms of vibrations and energy. I haven't asked him about my past lives or the dead who are still with me—it is this life so far I'm still assembling. I haven't mentioned the strong déjà vu I swim through when I visit Civil War battlefields.

I've decided to trust him on his clairvoyance but I have not yet decided to unguard when I talk about my lives outside of this one.

He once stuck a needle into my ear and when the needle set into the gristle of my ear I saw very clearly the view from the hospital window as my mother held me there a few hours after my birth. On the street below was my father and two sisters. My father was filming us with a Super 8 movie camera to save the moment of my mother waving with one hand and holding me with the other arm.

Haunted by Diebenkorn.
Haunted by Giacometti.
By NASA's Apollo missions.
Haunted by Antietam.

A photograph of Charles Duke and his family. Charles and his wife kneel behind their two sons in the backyard of their home in Houston. The older son wears a tie like his father wears.

There is a time when a son wants to be a man like his father is a man. There is a time when a son wants nothing else and then at some point anything other. Anyone other.

Charles Duke and his wife and sons posed in Houston. In 1972 Charles Duke put this photograph inside a plastic bag and taped it shut and he brought this photograph with him to the surface of the moon on Apollo 16 and there on the surface of the moon on the Descartes Highlands Charles Duke laid this photograph inside a plastic bag down onto the gray dust of the ground of the moon and stood back and took a photograph of the photograph on the moon. In the foreground is his bootprint and through the top left corner pass the tracks of the lunar rover.

Ophelia became upon another Hamlet. The first of him was dead. By annulling his words to her he etched out those vows and etched himself out as well.

Ophelia beholding a new Hamlet.
Get thee, though it was he who fled.
She wishes him restored.
The fugitive prince fugitive.

Ophelia's ultimate proposal is then to the reader to the seated to the globe to see what she sees. To see—is there no other way to witness this gone Hamlet?

My great aunt in Vermont slept with the lights on and when the lights were off the birds who flew and beat loud wings above her and when the lights were on the birds were gone.

"I haven't lived chronologically. No one does. Each moment reaches backward and forward to all other moments."
—Richard Avedon

I had it wrong that photograph of my father's house on Dead Horse Hill. The house instead was in Oxford Mass and not on Dead Horse Hill. It was the first house my grandfather owned, the downpayment put up by my grandfather's mother, my great grandmother. The ham radio shack was in the garage to the left of the house, outside the frame of the photograph.

For the house on Dead Horse Hill my father remembers the woods behind the house and walking there with his air rifle and Peach.

Backward to the woods, forward to the hunter.

The location of a tree near a brook. The cartography of threnody. Locate us in the ground of earth and then from there, from the facts of place and landmark, the sections and the grids and keys, we can leave.

My father's woods are known to me by my woods, the woods I mapped by stone walls and fallen ash and bends in where the water ran. The water ditch where the roots of a tree who fell came up and this ditch was shaded by those roots now standed up and veined. The color of the treaded paths in autumn who had a wet smell of the near end of what lives. I found things hidden by other boys inside stone walls and they could have found mine. The rock shelf who builded a line of shallow caves toward the low fields and the skunk cabbage in the muck where the water ended. There were paths to and in between this all, known by days among them.

How I see the woods where my father and Peach walked.
What I fill in where he couldn't say.

The painting of Ophelia by Millais is not a painting of Ophelia. The face of Ophelia is the face of a woman known to Millais, or a model laid back and looking upward for hours. She might have been the daughter of a patron. I could look this up.

What are the opposites of facts? Once it's written down it must be true, or as it comes to be in the writing.

Isn't there a story about Gertrude Stein and Picasso's portrait of her? When the portrait was done and shown to her she said the painting looked nothing like her. Picasso replied, "It will."

Don't worry, this is how you'll be known.

Three of them in a room. The painter, the model, the portrait. The artist, the author, the painting. Any one of them could have looked to the other two to see them, fond with difference.

Avedon's Giacometti. His right arm is behind his back and he's thinner from it. His eyes are off and seen over us and to his left. He seems about to say something or to walk forward and out beyond us to leave. He's dressed to leave not for his studio not for his work but still he is occupied with leaving.

Opposite Giacometti a monk hangs dead on a catacomb wall, mummified, capuchin, strings might hold his loose bones in place inside a gown around the bone of his upper arm and string tied around the bones above his wrist. His skull but a skull and hangs forward the holes where his eyes had once been now look down at the catacomb floor.

The dead hung lank and twigged.
Giacometti's Man Walking.
Giacometti coming forward.
Dovima's waist and her ilium out at us.

My father told me the name of his dog was Peach.
A German shepherd a stone fruit.

This was undone once. In a clearing. The correction of a photograph and in it the typed name of his dog. Peech, short for Pechacka, Greek for Peter.

Greek or Czech a rewrite.

"When the bird and the book disagree,
always believe the bird."
—John James Audubon

Haunted by Brancusi and Dix.
By Webern and Savannah.

"One small step for a man," and that was scripted and that was bungled.
"One small step for man," with his foot on the ground of the moon.
"For man" runs better in and then out of the mouth than "for a man"
which gets halted in the middle and stumbles.

A lingual correction, the aim undone.

We inherit our hairline from the father of our mother.
We all have this man about us.

There is a photograph of my mother's father. It is framed and it hangs in her house. He's in his early twenties and he's wearing a suit and tie and round steel-framed eyeglasses. The print is tinted somehow, not entirely grays and blacks but instead as if copper had something to do with the development.

I've been told I have his voice and when I say certain words in a certain tone it will give my mother a chill.

A chill is a signal from the body when a ghost is next to you.
A trade of heat in conjuring.

Avedon himself is to the left of her.
Marilyn looks off as if she's caught between attentions.

Her eyes are dull and half shut. She could be exhaling or about to speak. Her beauty is undiminished but it is, in this instant, paused.

A dear friend who lives in the desert has a found photograph of a woman sleeping. It's one of a series of prints he found, photos taken by a man, they might be on vacation, they might be inside the early days of quiet lust when it is all a wonder and it seems as if a new door has been kicked open inside you. There are prints of the woman standing smiling in a hotel room, sitting on the end of the bed, and there is a print of her sleeping.

Upon Marilyn we sense a trespass.

Avedon himself is alive and putting his hair in place.

Haunted by how Diebenkorn brought his figures and his land into the abstract.

I went alone to his retrospective.
I walked him chronologically.
In doing so it was clear his Ocean Park paintings are all landscapes.

I sat in the museum stairwell and I wrote this idea inside a notebook. How these landscapes went and left us but not without a map. Not without a shallow ridge where a toe could dig in and climb it up. I wrote this idea to make it true.

The more you close and open the notebook, the more you close and open and close and open and read again what you've put down the more true it is.

At some point I wanted for me what had Diebenkorn.
What's true is that I might still.

Feet can appear to be the roots of trees, veined.
A foot can depart like this.

I have a photograph of Baryshnikov I tore out of a magazine. It was an ad for leather bags. Sitting on the floor at his feet is Annie Leibovitz but she and the bags are left out of what I tore out. He's standing on a black wooden riser and his feet are bare and the toes of his left foot hang over the front edge of the riser.

His feet are almost unbelievable. They seem to be on their own a separate stone and each an uneven stone, each unmatched and rolling.

He said he was haunted by Fred Astaire. That all dancers are.

Feet can appear to be two fish. Feet can also appear to be the roots of trees or the two mounds who end a road.

Would it serve us to ask what part of us was handed down from the previous lives our parents lived?

I have heard Ireland is difficult to walk through because of this.

I'm told my family tree splits off and looking backward it runs into Scotland. Eighty years ago my grandmother could have told the story of her parents and their parents. It turns out genealogy is not so much a tree as it is the present record of an aspen colony.

If we are each or were at one time the rhizome who when traced back would find that early roots before us are now fled.

When I was young I would lay awake in bed and look at the faces in the top of the curtain. Is it called a plenum? That ruffle at the top who hides the curtain rod? In the creases when the light was off and there was only a side light coming in from the hall from a break in the door I saw faces with open mouths up in the plenum. They were looking down at me in my bed and had plans about me. I must have called for my father at some point. He came and lay beside me in the bed and I pointed out the faces in the plenum.

I had a photograph of my father. It was taken on the day of his graduation from the maritime academy. He's in the back row of a group of graduates. I don't know where that photograph is now. I can see his face clearly as it was that day.

It's not hard to believe the pheasant mounted on the wall of my father's office was once alive.
It's posed in flight.
Harder to believe is the desk where he always sat, the daybed behind him, the map under glass on the surface of the desk, the plastic model on a shelf above his radio bench of the Navy destroyer escort upon which he was underway.

Hamlet's father is a ghost who wants to speak but poultry keeps him silent for a bit.
The men at guard aim their pikes at an absence.

The director of *Hamlet* has a choice.
The ghost could be played by a man or not.
Not until scene five of act one does the ghost have any lines.
Enter Ghost and Hamlet.
I see Hamlet alone, walking alongside a voice.

To comfort him, Claudius tells Hamlet that all fathers die. And theirs. And that father lost, lost his. As if it could be no other way. As if the rules of loss have left us all here, as we are.

Gertrude tells her son that death is commonplace, ordinary. Accept it with the indifference of the men and women in Bruegel, so Berger. From Gertrude to Hamlet, Hamlet to thee.

Berger on Bresson's Giacometti,
how death has changed the artist.

I stumbled on Giacometti.
Stumbled on Noguchi.
I needed to believe it could all be learned.
Nature is our skeleton, the bones we drag around inside us.

If I didn't stumble on Giacometti. But there he was—a wheel
inside his feet. Or outside? The thin wasted vivid legs or not wasted but
pulled up to lift its head.
It all unfinished or so.
I couldn't enter as I wished.

I look it up and it's a chariot. Two big skinny wheels and a bench in between. I don't need to know what it could mean. But either way the tiny head is like a sun and all of it is resting. Going nowhere. Stayed to be seen and unbelieved.

Berger found Giacometti's death confirmed his work. And that his figures were made for himself, as observers of his future absence.

Nature is our skin. We buttress and apply, mark where the shadows go, and walk unfinished ahead. Until this also changes or falls away.

This Avedon who lets us choose. As if his portraits were something other than notes we found under rocks.

Marilyn can no longer be judged. Nothing is left to solve or decode.

When Rodin has decided a piece is done.
When Avedon has put a print in the frame.

I've never seen the photograph taken in spring in Boston I am facing her I am on the sidewalk beside a car she is standing inside the car she is up and through the open sunroof of the old sedan we are facing each other it is the North End of Boston it is spring we face each other there is no pause of us there is no end of us then.

I had a photograph of her. She sits with her back to the counter of the Blue Diner she sits on the edge of a counter stool her white t-shirt her cardigan her jeans her eyes were roads into me she spent the summer home in Edina. I was in Sturbridge with a photograph.

I slept unwell and I cut grass and I drove in cars to the lake and I slept one night on the sand by the ocean in Westerly and I set a field on fire who wouldn't douse and I never saw to it that anyone was well and I drove to a pond to work the summer.

I did not inherit clairvoyance. Or the ability to read and understand and question. Or how to look at art. Or generosity or forgiveness and sympathy.

I could ask my acupuncturist, the clairvoyant, if his skill was learned, or if it was inherited, or if it was handed to him by the dead.

Our predispositions. Our gifts. Our unshakeable ways. Our skeleton and what comes with it.

I listened to the jazz my father played in the house when I was young. And to the classical music he played in his office in the house. I was later drawn to Schoenberg and Webern and Stravinsky because they tore down what came before them and put up the new walls they felt. But not before I came to walk inside the halls of Beethoven and Vivaldi and Bach.

Clairvoyance must be a burden.
Or it might require that you become
more patient with the dead.

Builded by long gazing at Millais
the sunken Ophelia half-under.

Lighted by Berger's story, "The Brush."

By Kieslowski's *Blue*, Binoche in public pools in grief.

I dreamed I drowned last night I was in a public pool indoors it was a suburb in France the depth I was under near four stories and I looked up to the early evening light cast sideways lines down into the water up above me and I knew somewhere it was raining and above me she treaded there and wore a thin shift I swam upward those stories in between and I reached her in the silence of this I reached her foot and ankle and held her lightly enough to not pull her under and the joy of reaching her and holding on to her my heart it became larger inside me underwater I could breathe or at least there was no need to.

Our own story a deck of the misfiled acts we come across. Honesty is just the conviction of its assembly and gift or the delusion. I've misremembered my own life and shimmed it with the nearest study, the closest verse.

If there were a prologue and I wrote this prologue today it might have this in it.

That fathers never die and always die. That what haunts us walks along with us and photographs are false and also true. There are the living and the dead and the ones in between.

We come left to view this all and to measure what of it if it comes with us and to measure who left us there.

A prologue has certain facts and is bound in declaration. I no longer feel guided by opinions I've up to now hoven up. If there is some music in another room or coming from the next yard I'd go there to listen.

Best to let music have a stance.
What with all the questions posed there.

Who convinced us the dead no longer speak?

The Greeks and the ghost they use to stage the voices of the dead.

As if in death the speech of us is fled. Implied is that we listen only with ears but this is less than half of what we hear.

The Bell

In the near-last act of *The Passion of Andrei Rublev*, Boriska saves himself by convincing soldiers of the Prince that he knows the secret to casting a bronze bell. This secret, Boriska says, was handed down to him by his father when he was on his deathbed. The soldiers bring Boriska with them to the Prince instead of leaving him alone at the hut where the plague has killed off his family and where Boriska would have remained alone.

We learn the falsehoods later. The bell is cast and struck and the bell is true. Boriska risked beheading if the bell had failed but it did not. Exhausted he falls crying in cold mud and tells it seems no one that his father never gave him the secret of casting bronze bells. His father took it with him to the grave.

I'm unaware and unsure of Tarkovsky's moral here. Or even what facet of a man he wants us to view with him. But there is a part of me who believes Tarkovsky means for us to know that sons carry forward a father's knowledge whether this is intended or not. How could bones not carry the body he handed down?

The hands of all the women I've loved
The hands of my guides
The hands of teachers
Strangers

There was something like paper about my grandmother's hands
I might have a photograph of my grandmother in the basement
Inside a card
To see those hands
But it was the paper of them a photograph couldn't see again

Haunted by Rodin
The hands of each burgher

I struggle to pay attention enough to
seal these things away in me
But this is not a joyless challenge
I've begun befriending my forgetting

Wilkes-Barre and Savannah
Haunted by Lusk, Wyoming and Oxford
Eagle Nest and Eastern Oregon

"Photographic images have less visibility than the scenes they depict. "But photographs exert a force of coercion on the eyes which the visible scenes leave free. They are snakes for the eyes."
—Alphonso Lingis, on Mark Cohen

White three-story houses up the hillsides
of falling towns in winter side by each
close by the next the town in decline and
quiet unhelped into the present but left
in place each story a family and a porch

PART 2

The Rite of Spring: Adoration of the Earth

There is nothing soaring, nothing classically graceful or elegant, the tutus gone and instead loose overdresses of what could be coarse bolts, the slippers or pointe shoes gone and instead plain sandals laced up the calf, each step in this choreography pounding into the earth each dancer, arms and hands pushed downward to the ground, the bodies of the dancers rarely upright but instead in loping hunch it seems there must be something larger hung above them and their refuge is in the earth.

In Part One, an ancient woman describes the future in a hunched route of stomps and circles.

In Part Two, hides hung over them who stalk or they affirm the one who is stood and still. The chosen one. Her stillness becomes an object. It isn't possible to look away from her stillness, the courage of her stillness, the skill of this.

When she stands unmoving in the center of a turning field she stands askew one shoulder lifted and her eyes are set down onto the floor and she is pigeon-toed and garish but still.

Did Nijinsky draw this carriage? About this bended branch did Nijinsky leave notation?

Or is this an interpretation, a read, a channeling from elsewhere into the present a new stillness? What a body does inside the dance but not of it.

I could look this up, whether Nijinsky left a sketch or if he left choreography how to hide or how to be unseen.

Nijinsky died in a madhome. This exit is now obsolete.

We pray to the dirt of where we're from. As if in prayer we can somehow disclose who we are. This is our shorthand. Our surest tell.

Pounding the earth with our wander, kneading the dirt of where we're from, garish in the disguise we use against the notion that we all might be ordinary, an accident of the elements.

"I made the great mistake of returning to my hometown after not being anywhere near the place for over forty-five years...Why would anyone volunteer to take a stroll through their distant past other than to torture some memory of a long-lost counterpart."
—Sam Shepard, from "Four Days"

But the going back is builded in. As if the concert of our bones is not already scripted.

When I was eight I hiked with four or five other boys from the neighborhood into the woods behind the house where my family lived. I was the youngest on the hike and at an age when age and seniority determined a strict rank among us. I rarely spoke and had little confidence among the older boys but I wanted nothing more than to be among them. We packed sandwiches and apples and we had a couple metal Boy Scout canteens. These canteens had canvas covers you could run your belt through and wear the canteen like an army man at your waist and it made an important clanging sound when you walked and the water in the canteen splashed against the metal walls. We walked out back across a field of milkweed and then across McGilpin Road and into the woods on a trail who might have been used by hunters. I don't remember if much was said as we walked. We crossed what we called the powerline which was a natural gas right of way and it was a straight clear-cut in the woods a hundred feet wide and miles long. Beyond the powerline we picked up another trail and walked single file. We stopped for lunch more out of ceremony than hunger. We ate our lunch in the woods and we had carried our lunch to this place in the woods. We later walked through a swampy part of the woods where skunk cabbage bloomed and it smelled wet. One of the boys went to pick a strange flower but Marty, the oldest, told him to stop. Don't pick that flower, he said. It's a lady slipper. It's illegal to pick them. Marty told us how rare these flowers were and that only a handful were on the planet and men have gone to jail for picking them. We all came in closer to look at the odd cup-shaped thing on the floor of the woods. It was mostly white with streaks of dark red and red spots. There was silence as we looked at the lady slipper. We walked farther into the woods and the trail came out on a small paved road and it turned out that we had walked to Southbridge, the next town over. We turned around and walked back home with Marty in the lead.

My father sailed in the U.S. Navy between the years of the Korean War and the war in Vietnam. He was commissioned on a destroyer escort and took liberty in ports on the Mediterranean.

He said of the places he'd been the Greek islands were the most beautiful.

He also mentioned Rimini. Or Bimini.

Once in Morocco or Libya he went with a couple of his shipmates into the port city and walked through a street market. He said there was a man there wearing a turban and the man was doing tricks of some kind. My father called this man a fakir and said he also had a monkey and at some point in the show the fakir threw a rope into the air and the rope stayed there suspended while the monkey climbed up the rope and then climbed down and when the fakir lowered his arms the rope fell back down to earth. My father wasn't able to explain how this happened or even how he could have been fooled into seeing something that was not there at all.

Sailing across the Atlantic Ocean the seas were once so high that envelopes inside the mailroom's mail slots, which were angled downward at forty-five degrees to keep the mail in place, were falling out onto the mailroom floor the ship was listing as much.

I saw myself in Morocco. I might have been in Navy whites the tropical long whites for liberty. The market is crowded and the details of this are borrowed from a film or television or news images of crowded Middle Eastern markets where vendors sat on woven rugs with baskets around them and people walked between the rugs and baskets and vendors and all bodies were in contact with something on every side. What I wore was from a photo I'd seen of my father. The fakir has a space around him as room is always builded around a street performer how a crowd can come to an understanding of this. We work together in this and I move to see the fakir and to keep from being in the way and I see the rope climb into the air and how it stands straight up and as if the bottom of the rope was more stable than the top the monkey held on to the bottom of the rope to test it and then the monkey went up the rope as quickly as it would seem possible and as quickly came down feet first and the fakir who had his arms up brought them down and his thin sleeves fell which was a signal to the rope to come back down from where it had been held there by a spirit his assistants who held the rope from inside the sky. I walk around as if a different angle would betray his legerdemain but I was no better off behind him. In the air above him there was no point from which he could have fastened a fishing line I looked up into the place above him and there was only the blue that I had seen in pictures of Morocco.

Family of Origin is a term used in therapy to describe an individual's first caretakers and siblings or the first social group of which an individual is a part.

It is believed your Family of Origin cuts your first record, the one you have on repeat until you die. How aware you are of the grooves is the trick a therapist will try to teach you.

The last time I met with my clairvoyant acupuncturist I was scheduled to meet with him for ninety minutes. We talked for the first thirty minutes and he mentioned something about my profession which led me to understand he thought I was someone else sitting there with him. For thirty minutes he thought I was someone else. After I reminded him who I was we continued, but for the rest of our session I was distracted by the thought that it was somehow possible for a clairvoyant to not know who was sitting across the room from him.

The Family of Origin is one way to describe the maps we're born with. Our predispositions and mental legacies. Our further back than that. The abusers in the rhizome who handed down their charts and roots. The shadow guest who knows a grandfather took his life in the woods in the snow with his gun.

In my grandparents' basement there was an old television who took a long time to warm up and it was on for me and my sisters. I don't remember what was on the television at the time but I got up from where I was sitting and I walked up to the television screen and crying I hit the screen with both hands pounding on the screen and crying. There was a taste in the back of my mouth like putty or clay and there was the sense that I could smell the clay inside my face. There was also the sensation that my hands and fingers were enormous and swollen and if I touched my thumb to a finger it would make a muffled clicking sound like two rocks who tap under water. What I remember next was my mother holding a cold cloth on my forehead, I was lying on the pinkish couch and I was still bothered by something but there was a period of time in there now lost. I don't believe it was ever mentioned again and I've never asked again about it. I have a feeling they'd all rather not recall it in the way a family can understand a wound but keep it well unsaid. The better angels tell me it's been forgotten and only I replay the track.

Behind my grandparents' house was the ham radio shack my father built. It had a checkered linoleum tile floor and framed pictures on the wall of men gathered around ham radios in stiff poses and of elaborate aerial antennas. It smelled of grease or oil and I spent hours in there alone, looking through boxes in the quiet shack, paging through old check stubs and road atlases, piecing something new together from the discard.

My grandmother was haunted by a styrofoam head used to store a wig. Soon after this she was moved into a group home on a hill in Worcester.

On walks around our neighborhood in Stamford my father and I would pass by the house of an old woman who paced back and forth on her front porch and she moaned in a way that described some great loss. My father told me she had snapped her twig. I tried to picture what this meant and this also was an early view into what I thought was where we all finish.

Avedon's asylum portraits
As if the pairing is with itself
The body near able
And the eyes turned inward to view
the bested self

Haunted by those odd towns who have buried in them an uncounted procession of histories of each soul's tromp through childhood and youth and anguish and peace and the merits gathered and them who left and them who remained and remain and the charts of mothers who keep true calendars who chart the upcoming days in red pencil and bury dead angelfish in backyards for daughters unaware they build a charnel ground beside the house and those bodies remain there like bookmarks left in works too thick to finish.

Odd towns beside old battlefields what haunts is up and beside us. How walking through Ireland is difficult on account of the ghosts who wander there and the sure parade of them. I've heard this about Ireland and I know this about Wilkes-Barre and Fredricksburg and Vicksburg and in Wyoming in the town of Lusk.

The land we use to board our dead. How we tend to those finished overcoats. How a burglar was thrown down a well head-first and his children lived into old age.

Ralph Steadman draws Arnold Schoenberg.
Picasso paints Gertrude Stein.

Some wars have swallowed poets. Or all of them.

He was oddly proportioned. I've read this about Nijinsky. I've read other things about Nijinsky. His madness is what took over in the end. If I remembered more about Nijinsky I'd write it out for you but I've forgotten what I read about his letters and his wife and the man he lived with before his wife and his madness and the hospital where he was committed and the letters he wrote from there.

When I swim in a pool or a lake I like to float on my back with my lungs full and my ears under the waterline so I can breathe and remain there and I can smell the land and I can see up into what's there to see and there is a soft cup on top of what I hear so the sound is almost gone except what I hear with my mouth or the clicks of things through the water and it is here I feel I have no obligations or even others in my life at all as if closing off a sense won't allow it.

There is surrender in Ophelia's expression. Unattached and in the brook she could be on about allowing herself to let her light out under the waterline.

What's handed down and what haunts us.
Fathers never die on account of this.

What's handed down is an ear who builds up a sound and eyes who raise any light, a fear of being photographed, mistrust in the saved image, mistrust in halted time, a fear of solitude and of change, fear of abandonment and a belief there are no allies, no sympathizers, no assistance.

In the minutes before a body dies the color under each fingernail turns from pink to blue.

In the moments before a body dies the breathing becomes irregular and the space between each breath is drawn out and this space is measured in up to half-minutes and so the body's final breath is known only to itself for a brief time. This pause the body's final sleight of hand.

My father's stepfather, Godfrey, took apart an old furnace so it could be removed from the basement. The walls of the furnace were heavy and there were thick layers of asbestos between the outer and inner walls and Godfrey broke these walls apart with a sledgehammer. A couple decades later my father watched his stepfather die of lung disease in a hospital in Worcester, Mass. My father said he saw the moment when the color fell from his face and he became gray and left us.

The word for room in Italian is *camera*.

Tarkovsky carried with him a Polaroid camera and he took instant photographs in Italy not so much for continuity but instead to put a halt to what he saw and what he saw was always moving.

Tonino Guerra, in a book of Tarkovsky's instant photographs, tells the story of Michelangelo Antonioni who took an instant photograph of three Muslim elders in Uzbekistan. After handing over the photograph the elders considered the image and one of them asked, "Why stop time?"

Andrei Tarkovsky left Russia to make his films in Italy. When a deep illness took up inside him he requested that his wife and son visit him before he died but this request was denied. Eventually his son, Andrei Jr., was allowed to leave Russia to visit his dying father who was then in France.

There is a photograph of Tarkovsky in his last days in France. He's lying in bed, propped up so he can see the room he's in. A small bird is near his left hand. In his room there is a tall window behind him. In his last days this small bird flew into his room in the morning through the open window and landed on the bed of the dying film director.

There is no interpretation to give this story any added color or meaning. It is a small bird in France, in the morning, visiting a man near death who can only move gently.

I overheard a man telling a story. His wife came home and after entering the house she noticed a woman sitting in a chair in the living room. The woman was older and unfamiliar. The man's wife was unsure what to do and so she waited a moment, blinked her eyes, and after blinking her eyes the woman was gone.

He then listed some of the previous residents of their house. Former renters and owners and how long each of them had lived there. He also mentioned that the chair in the living room in which the older woman was sitting was recently acquired at a yard sale. There was something scientific about the way he mentioned these facts, as if they were part of a well-known empirical set of data used to explain such occurences. The mathematics of the paranormal.

We don't put up with open ends. The unexplained unbearable. Would you be more at ease to know the spirit of the former owner of the armchair in your living room was casting and unsettled downstairs?

I wish I had been taught to befriend the dead. But instead we pick this up alone, when the occasion demands it, and we bring to this occasion what we believe is useful and we consider ourselves prepared but we are not.

I rode in the car with my mother to stores in downtown Stamford. I rode in the far back seat of the station wagon when my mother drove me to nursery school in Greenwich. I went with my mother to pick up my sisters at ballet practice from Mrs. Pollard's.

I rode in the car with my mother from Stamford to Sturbridge in heavy rain and the windshield wipers were on as fast as they could be on the entire way through the night.

We drove to Southbridge to buy school clothes. We drove to Worcester where my mother worked in a clothing store for pregnant women and I would stay there with her for hours and each clothing rack was circular and each rack was a fort I could go into between the clothes.

When I could drive my mother and I would drive to Maine and walk on beaches and in Camden and Rockport.

Recently I drove my mother to the hospital and then a few days later I drove her to lunch. Through neighborhoods and past buildings we'd driven by two hundred times. Overcast. No lights. Us sitting side by each.

How color can be used to hide a thing and color is also what depicts the details, the notes in between the lines.

The word is valance I was looking for, not plenum, the curtains along the top who hide the rod. The ruffles of the valance are what hid the faces there and those faces came with mad plans upon me.

My father lying in bed there with me and we looked up at the valance and the shadows in it. The faces disappeared when we looked at them together and when he left they must have reappeared but I can't remember. The memory ends with my father lying in the bed with me. As if a memory needs the bones of a story to be salvaged.

The bones and the colors to add depth and detail to what's told, or the color who in a drab wash conceals what might have been told after the end.

What we choose to carry, or what we haven't shed.

The disjointed movies of what we passed through, a glance a curtain a pattern of a dress the light the way it lit us from the television us on the carpet on the floor the light made us blue my hand on her blue the mornings slept in and the clouds above a city the woman in Europe who sold a rock hammer the splinter from a deck the zinnias saved inside a plastic terrarium the smell of matches burned the smell of autumn.

This is what we choose to lug with us among endless scraps. The worn-out phrase about the cutting room floor but isn't that the lion's share of what we set about in us and to call this freight anything more precious than accidental would be a trick a false coin.

We bargain with us. We stay away from plants who make us melancholy.

My stepmother is not the only survivor to be visited by the recent dead in the form of a cardinal bumping up against a window to try to make it through the glass.

Tarkovsky knew it wasn't so much the contents and continuity of the scene that was important—the rooms and walls and colors and actions—but instead the most important part of a scene was the lingering emotional and visceral mood the scene conveyed. It might appear to be a scene from another film unrelated, married only by the sound of water dripping in a cold room, but the almost unnameable quality of the scene, the residual atmospheric charge, is what Tarkovsky knew was the true measure and import of the scene.

Wake up from a dream on the verge of crying or enraged and what's remembered from the dream is not the story but only a recollection of the color of the sand hill or the way a dress fell. Tarkovsky's Polaroid pictures are rent from dreams and exist as proof we live unattached to our own story.

Our Polaroids uncollected.

I was ill and she turned around to see me as the car drove her away.

My dog Gravy in the tall grass of a field by a reservoir in Vermont.

Did I mention that my father took a picture of the fakir in Morocco? At the moment when the monkey was climbing the rope that hung up in the air by only itself my father took a picture with a camera. Or it might have been a shipmate who did this.

When the film was developed there was the photograph of the fakir and the crowd gathered there in Morocco and the photograph showed the fakir with his arms raised and to one side to present what was there to the crowd gathered and to his side where the rope should have been and where the monkey should have been instead to his side up into the air where his raised arms presented there was nothing. There was nothing on the other side of the photograph and there was nothing on the negative slide held up to the sun. There were no other photographs on the roll with something missing.

When I was ill she turned around in the back seat to see me through the back window as the car she was in drove away. She left me with the photograph of her sitting on a stool at the Blue Diner, her back to the counter. When she was two years old she wore a tiny kimono and sat on a couch in Edina with an open book in her lap and her eyes on the pages and a photograph of this she left with me as well.

I heard that Buzz Aldrin snapped his twig after he returned from the Apollo missions. I tried to confirm this but I could not.

Buzz Aldrin and Neil Armstrong took hundreds of photos while they walked on the surface of the moon. There are several photographs of Buzz Aldrin on the surface of the moon, taken by Neil Armstrong. Buzz Aldrin did not take any photos of Neil Armstrong on the surface of the moon.

The sunken roads near Antietam Creek and Sharpsburg when they are wet and the ruts are filled with dark water and the afternoon light is at such an angle that it gives the impression the near saplings and vines and deep green thick bushes will grow and overtake what has been cleared and the trees keep all this in place and the canopy of the trees is a good house up above to match this with the woods of where we come from the home woods and sunken roads the clearings and the worn path the deer made the boys walk on and name it something new again we understand the woods we read about through our own woods the creeks by our own creeks the smoke we read about the smoke who climbs up from the pages we lit on fire inside a rock circle in the woods.

The term schizophrenia was coined in Zurich in 1911.

Nijinsky's last public appearance was in Montevideo in 1917 performing with Arthur Rubenstein for a Red Cross benefit. Nijinsky was twenty-eight and showing signs of mental decline, had been suffering nervous breakdowns, and he would be diagnosed schizophrenic soon afterward. Nijinsky danced some steps to Chopin. It is said that Rubenstein cried in his presence.

In 1919, Nijinsky gave a final dance performance for an invited audience of wealthy patrons and royalty at the Suvretta House in St. Moritz. By the account of Nijinsky's wife Romola, he began the performance by sitting in a chair facing the audience, and he sat there staring at the audience for nearly a half hour. He then said, "Now I will dance you the war… The war which you did not prevent."

In his madness, Nijinsky locked himself in his studio and worked for uninterrupted hours on his new dance notation and he made countless ink drawings, most of which were pairs of eyes looking off into the corners of the page or looking back at you.

My grandfather walked into the woods behind the house where he rented rooms he had a gun he lay down on his back onto the snow.

I brought her to the airport in Boston and she flew home to Minneapolis. I don't remember saying goodbye or how at all we parted. On the train back to Kenmore Square and then walking up Commonwealth Avenue I felt inside a sensation that gathered loss and lust and an ache for something missing like a hollowness below my collarbones with a sense of wealth and with a loss of self with an acceptance that I had given some of what I was away. This must have been March or April and it was warm in the sun and I stood on the sidewalk in the sun and was overtaken by this flood who ran through me from my head down through the floor of me and I stood in the warm sun to believe in it.

A friend who had flown home to Michigan had left his apartment window unlocked for me and I walked to his apartment to the back porch and climbed through the window into his bedroom. It was quiet inside his room and there was the sound of the city outside but it was distant and soft and I was alone in what I now know in looking back on this was the first of an adult solitude I came to relish and also later came to fear for what it often led to. I lay on the bed with my head on my friend's pillow and I held the emptiness of where she was not and I saw her dark eyes and her black hair make a room for us with her face above mine and her black hair hung down around us there was only that one room and the planet became a planet out from there. The city sounds near mute and a warm patch on the bed where the sun landed and the city whoever continued continued around me.

Sebald wrote long sentences on Corsica. The winding hilly paths who led him to the sea and his difficult swim there.

He said the dead haunt Corsica. Wealthy Corsicans were given a formal ceremony and were interred while the poor were thrown down a hole that was something like a well. The bodies down inside the hole stacked and rotting. The record of a town in settled bones.

In Corsica when the dead returned they were about a foot shorter than when they were alive and sometimes instead of legs and torsos there would be just the waving dance of mist or smoke and there never was sure detail of the face or head.

These are old accounts.
But accounts of the dead do not expire.

It's hard to believe the math of our bones is already written.

I've seen a picture of my father standing with his grandmother in Springfield, Mass. He's wearing a new leather jacket and there is a smile on his face as sincere as any I've seen. My father is about fifteen years old and his grandmother had just taken him clothes shopping in Springfield.

From what I can tell these trips to Springfield were uncommon and from what I've seen in pictures also uncommon was that smile.

It's a miracle we make it as far as we do.
A miracle we have as many days as we do.
A miracle we see to others
after the astound of our own salvage.

PART 3

[William Eggleston | Untitled]

I've been the pictured, backseated and between lives, hauling the past along but ahead I'm not encumbered. I'm light tomorrow. New plates new state new stare leaving something someone expects him returning. Watched as we've all been watched with a try to be alone inside the seen.

Self-scribbled his sharpened pen dug in his arm a mudded icon we have the sign posts in us, on us, we hide best our own hints into what's upcoming. I'm well I'm not well I bring the hallway of this limbo along with me. Backseated driven poised in his about to be. Or held against his own study, some plan who had no ending well.

What's best for the body is not running miles or lifting barbells from where they rest or fasting or drinking only nut milk for a week or stretching but what's best for the body is to rise and move and continue to move. His long thumbnail. Hinds County, Mississippi. The county of Jackson, Clinton, Pocahontas and Cayuga. East of Vicksburg and the bluffs there and Grant's siege.

If you catalog what you see, if that's something you do, you'd enter a pink hand-dyed shirt and that unclean, dark pants pinstriped in red and white, silver rings, bracelets or one bracelet wound a few times of leather or dark beads, thick eyebrows thick hair and mustache, the rounded glass of the back window and behind this all a flatfender Jeep, a Mississippi license plate in Hinds County his new license plate, and you'd enter the longer thumbnail for the reason of guitar or for another reason, and you'd enter the straight stare ahead. His body what of it is aware of Eggleston. How to look when asked not to look.

[William Eggleston | Untitled]

The back seat as a prison, for example. They sit captured, captive. At the mercy—the mercy, at once in generosity and at once the warder the one with the keys the key out the key forward. Eggleston himself is seated in the front and shoots from his station of vice warder but the ones there backseated don't see him as such it seems it could be his eyes before the camera comes up his eyes could play the more benign role of mercy. The ones backseated seem held gently in a kind of bargained willingness.

City syndromes. We love our captors, our captors love us in return. He said something about his best friend who no longer is alive because he was hit on the head with an axe. This proves a photograph does not stand in the way of anything. Might a photograph even hasten what's to come? There's no way to look this up but arranging a test for it would be worth the while. This is not a question of philosophy but instead of how the light moves through a room or through the windows of a rested car.

[William Eggleston | Untitled]

If you catalog what you see if you were one to notice and log what's there you'd note how the windows when both the front seat window and the back seat window are rolled down there is no pillar remained and what was once called a hard top convertible you'd note the man and his glasses and his hand holding a corn stalk up against the back door he's looking down at the man who all we see of him are his legs raised up and his feet resting on the side of the car below the passenger door handle you'd note the shade on them both and on the long white car it couldn't be known what brought them here or how it came to pass that one man took to lying in the grass with his feet up on the car.

The photograph itself is a record a log of one moment between two moments, two moments at large on the timelines before and after, moments at large and then pinned down by the edges.

The back seat as a carrel in between moments. In transition but at the mercy of others. The phone booth, the hotel bed the mixed drink on the airplane table next to the rounded corner window the diner stool the way a man or woman sits alone and this indicates a temporary stasis in the continuous and aleatory migrations from here to there from there to there.

PART 4

“When people look at, say, a portrait of somebody, we always think that what we’re saying is, ‘This person is no longer.’ But in fact, it’s the other way. It’s us that do not exist for that photograph.

“And as such, there is a grief, a mourning of the loss of—always built into a photograph. On my painting table, I have a photograph of Robert Frost with his son, Carol. And Carol, many years after that photograph—in the photograph, Carol is maybe 13. Many years later, Carol committed suicide. And I have that photograph with two apples from Robert Frost’s orchard on my painting table. And I look at it every day, and I think: That photograph knew everything that was to come, sort of in the leaning of Carol toward his father—the future was there. And I look at it every day to figure out if I can catch it, and which part of it.”

—Enrique Martinez Celaya, from an interview with Krista Tippett

In *The Americans* by Robert Frank is a photograph with the title "Elevator—Miami Beach." What Miami Beach there is of it is only guessed in the blurred stole on the shoulders of a woman exiting the elevator car and outside the elevator in what could be the glare of sunlight or the brightness of a polished hotel lobby the indistinct shape of the leaves of some decorative plant that seems to have large out-facing leaves on a rounded perimeter. A man, also blurred and unlit, still inside the elevator car and he's in motion toward the open door and all we can see of him is his silhouette, the glasses on his round head and the line of the leading edge of him. What is in focus is the woman working in the elevator dressed like a bellhop with a white garishly fastened waistcoat and she stands against the panel where all the buttons are lined up. Her left hand is tucked in at her waist it seems to lean it on the button that keeps the elevator door open, open for the silhouette and his glasses. This lean appears to be second nature, the lean again into the panel when the doors open where the buttons know where to be the lean again the button her hand between the button and her belly where it feels good to be aware of when a hand is rested there. But in the middle of the field is her gaze set inside what I've imagined, through the flawed lens of my own melancholy and the countless misplaced assignments of another's composure and the countless misreads of another's body settled into what it knows and knows how to fall and rest in place and through the unended guesses as to how another person at all continues through the footfalls and the echoes of a day intact and braided well enough to keep on, is an exhaustion only fended by what her gaze is landing on and even then it's not so much the object of her gaze but what she's builded for herself as a mystic empties herself to the object of deep study and finds herself gone, dismembered, or rather without substance much at all and remains there as a single witness to this landscape solely inward and perfected by these hours of careful abeyance. But what of her expression and the way the dark middles of her eyes hang upward like dark circles floated to the tops of her eye whites and the lifted eyebrows and how the corner of her painted mouth angles down and seems resigned or rather unable to play along any longer? One life held to attest to the moments just before and just after.

And if the photograph does know everything that is to come, what would the bones of it read? What would the lean against the panel wall say about the upcoming days? What would the shadow on her remarkable nose divine?

THE HISTORY OF MY SURNAME

The moon a low dish and a ship hauls them through the night. Karl Axel and Axel Herman his son and Georg his brother among the quiet fled. They stare out at the gapless sea to allow the world its unfolding. Some few placed by their faith in the hands of God and set to unfurl the mysteries of his guidance through devoted reading and a hoisting here and there of choice verse. Though most of the fled have gone headlong into kegs of whiskey such that it seems the shouting and the donnybrooks and the rolling anthems are somehow captured in the keg itself and come released without fail with the prying of the bung. Karl Axel among the floored for his decision has set him out into a vast sea which if he pitched himself over the rail would not pause or change at all in the swallowing but instead continue its great unquilted heaving. Mist from the heavy dips raised upward in cloud shapes. The hull weight massive and mist a fleet air steady in its beat and gone as quick.

In steerage his son appears slept but in truth the rhythm of the ship though not unlike the sway of his mother walking with him clung to her sides builds an unsettle in him from the cold bigness of the rock and sway. The closed eyes unbetray his inner mood. To see the sleeping child one is calmed in the vision but to know his young regards would paint darker rooms. Surrounded in close by other goers and leavers and those freighted down by who remains on land. The son a tight ball, knees drawn in and corded by his new arms. The good smell of home who lives inside the wool blanket. Across the thin aisle a woman watches him, her look that of someone shot through with hollow.

~~~~~

A line on the death of Gustava Persson

Twenty nine days after the birth of Gustava Karolina the mother Gustava bended over for the air no longer held her up but instead she came to find that she was made of air and that inside her head some bees and the sound of all her bees inside the air that made her up was the sound of a body who gets lifted away as it sleeps and so in bed tumbled down with risen heat come to cook her from the insides out and work the bees into an all on susurrus Gustava wife of Axel son of Per now built of only air and the sound of bees went up and died.

~~~~~

Through Sweden on canals dug by men, earth moved and water took its place in a clean row and locks to lift or settle ships into the flatness. Another ship to England where Karl Axel and Axel Herman and Georg for a week remain in London at the Scandinavian Sailors Temperance Home, sailing in to London past the tattered fishing boats rigged with oilcloth sails like no few dirty sacks floated there and hope was missing from these boats. Loaded up again by train to Gravesend where they board the *Ruapehu* charted south to bend under the Cape of Good Hope and east to Australia.

Six days out and the island of Tenerife which to the eye is a cloud at first but nearing it grows stones and high peaks and here they take on coal from barges come up alongside the *Ruapehu*. Men of filth from Spain and Portugal and Italy come on board to remove their top clothing and carry sacks of coal on their deep-colored backs and smoke tobacco, one square in the mouth and another crammed on the ear lit with the final drag of the square before. The coal men stop for dinner and their spread is the color of fruits carved by thin pocket knives and bread is lopped off as such and they drink wine from bottles the cork tied to a string. They end their dinner with tobacco and haul again on their backs the coal that paints their skin.

Karl Axel and young Axel Herman and Georg ferry on to the island of Tenerife where clean white houses climb the hills around Santa Cruz and a mountain covered in vines is up through the clouds. They buy two buckets of fruit and wine. They rent a guide who vends a trail to the cave of the hermit Saint Alonzo and they all four follow a rude cut in the hillside up out of town through a saddle and into where the sun shines brightly in a steep valley. Inside the cave they walk their hands along the walls polished smooth by other pilgrims who came to witness the dark place where Alonzo spent his life in silence. They rest inside the cave. Their breathing is the only sound they hear. But soon the ghosts inside the cave grow tired of the heavy breathing and chase out the wandered Swedes into the daylight.

Walking back, the sounds of any day intruding now as bells and horns might. But it's only birds and their own hard footsounds. Then this too recedes. On deck the *Ruapehu* again all bustled and commote. Heading south into the rising hotness of a day unknown in Sweden.

His muscles are sore from the scrabbling they did and Karl Axel lays hands upon his son's back and shoulders so to work out from in them what his own shoulders carry. He kneads the young tendons and the muscle. Lying behind young Herman on their bunk Karl Axel pours into the boy what healing from his hands he can muster and in doing so there is builded a belief in his hands and for the gift they dole.

Passing through the equator on deck Karl Axel crams a knife into a decking joint for his son and brother and self to view what no shadow falls from it. A tailwind steady with the ship and hotness grows. A worn stoker is brought up from below.

From Capetown for a week the *Ruapehu* is woven to the rivets in a family of waves unended and severe. The hull's dip a steel bobbin gone tucked under by the side waves who break entire like bended clouds or whole drifted ponds. Most on board become ill. And there is the notion of smallness on a globe unworried for a single ship or its final port. The scale of all their seeing pulled through a famous lens. Then calmness struck and resurrected all save few who harbored in them yet a tossing remnant and who could know if their inner weather wasn't taut for good.

Against the weather was a concert in which ten waiters used coal dust to change their outlook and they were enjoyed that night and the night upcoming. From Capetown southeast driven down a sidewind menaced the ship fro in heeling, such a list gone steep a body didn't stand a chance without some grip or rail. Southeast toward the Crozet Islands about which an ask is builded into all such passing ships to survey the risen land there in the chance these remotes harbor men whose strand has prisoned them. The twin hope to not find and to find a crew stuck. To not find was the *Ruapehu*'s luck so east as east can chart. A fortnight's beeline. The wind a steady throwback. The roaring longitude living to its name and with this ever back breeze in assist the *Ruapehu* barges on due east into the long unbroken heart of the voyage. In snow for days a mid-sea blizzard hounds full upon them. Makes the world a world inside itself or like a smaller version with inside it only sea and one ship dusted. Axel and Georg compare ideas on what could be much less at all than what they are on board the ship just then.

In daytime undeterred by how the weather pockets them a band of English cause a running race. The race includes the uncorking of soda water and to finish without a touch of the bottle to the mouth. Circuits of the ship's rear lounge excelled at by one enlivened priest whose speed of foot reminded them in witness of a hunting dog and whose acumen to finish bottles conjured Uhlin's beer house in Lervik. Another challenge on deck saw men in crouch tied at the wrist and a rule laid down in chalk.

Nineteen days in such an eastern course whose sole vantage the open sea whose sole rhythm the engines below and days from light to dark and back. Then land was spotted and ahoyed, the passengers coming up from below along the rail their no few languages declaring beauty upon Tasmania.

Georg on a bunk inside the hold. Below him Karl Axel and Axel Herman, the father outlining the son their bodies one coiled about the smaller. Little sunlight touches them. Coal dust and tobacco smoke have changed the essence of their wool blanket that once housed the notion of from where they come. Axel Herman the son of Karl Axel and Gustava, his mother gone of fever his infant sister Gustava Karolina left in the care of an aunt—these threads back to his Sweden most fragile. The memories builded in him are like a spider's net, unseen at first but given time and dust become more revealed. His past a play in the garden of the stories inside us and the heart.

Joiners for a year Karl Axel and Georg learn Japanese timber joints full common in Australia. They vend and ply this trade until Georg plans for them to fish and gets them in tow behind the *Hawea* to pull their own fishing boat the *Venture* to Port Campbell.

"This undoubtedly referred to two brothers named Persson who had decided to commence fishing operations in Port Campbell."

—Portland Guardian

Karl Axel ends his final letter to the Söderhamns Tidning in Sweden with this sentence: "To eradicate the sparrow a shooting premium is paid."

Heavy sea at the quay outside Port Campbell runs the brothers and the *Venture* toward the east reef and the breakers there. An immense sea tops the *Venture* broadside and leaves her hull-up, the brothers Karl Axel and Georg in cling to the upturned hull, their keeled hands an only hope. From the *Hawea* a corked rope floats out toward the east reef but the making swell unallows the *Hawea* such a closeness for to reach them with it. The swell continues and unrelents upon the brothers clung there to the hull. The sea is too enraged to send rescue boats against it so Port Campbell watches the hull and the two men thereupon it and the sea who means to land the brothers. At dusk the green hills of Port Campbell fetch the glow of this fled day and from the nearest hill it's noticed that only one man now clings to the tossing hull. At dawn there is no man and there is no hull and pieces of the *Venture* wash up onto the beaches at Port Campbell.

Axel Herman is five years old. It is unknown what he is told about the sea and how the sea came up and through no plan took off for good his uncle and his father.

~~~~~

A line on the love of Axel Herman

She was sended down from hidden spas the globe her cherrystone and her work was a feather up against the skin we shed and then her strong heart one morning came into a flourish gone mad inside its own madness like two painted birds gone berserk for the same kivver, in a shallow pool they went waded side by each and then the pool teetered on its hinge and left them up against it there to wrestle with the notion of entire versus half and with the notion of a world who gives or one who rips away and to wrestle with each other.

~~~~~

A line on the death of Axel Herman

Suited as he is for Munson Trade School and the walk he's done for scores of years in deep set winter inside his woolen coat and hat the day full clear and early sunlight banks off the snow at hand as such Axel Herman bundled gets to school his olden skin a thin cold paper wrap until the warm of his one classroom ends the chill and setting down his coat and then his hat he sits down at the desk he knows and feels the tingle when hands who go from cold to warm again regain their blood and tingles follow through the limb it so occurs this feeling and upward like a slow gone beetle carries volts and numbness up his arms and soon his whole entire is a volt and shotted numb so Axel Herman puts his head down on his desk for god damn he might just need a piece of rest is all.

THE HISTORY OF EGON SCHIELE IN PRISON

In my own power I've come and of my choosing which is not true. This gaol is a room to me and I embrace it also this is not true. Washed in white the sides of it, the split floorboards gone into the polish of a foot down slid upon it for years and again. What a tank a stove they laid. I will be the one to refill the tinder box and the one who stokes a heat duly. My narrow cot, the woolen sheet set and where the white wall meets the wool bedding is like any beach, two grand loves hove up to the other and fendless exist stood up straight and each good.

Wally has been allowed in and I study close her eyes for how to spend my hope. Wally is in the world and can hear what I do not. Her dear senses and her eyes. So I draw from them the meaning or the guess she carries in her body. How she sits toward me or the fall of her shoulders. I ask her to bring to me some pencils and the paper which has already gotten readied and to bring some color as it is each day the work of the day to steady a self against the white walls and the corners of the walls and the black stove.

I have a chair and which it could be set down inside the floor we share. My chair. I commend you as you've been set. You hold fast and I model me after you.

Wally has returned with paper and with the colors and pencils and her eyes betray how gaunt I am and I am there for her. I brought myself risen to the day. It was Wally brought also an orange against the hunger and against the quiet.

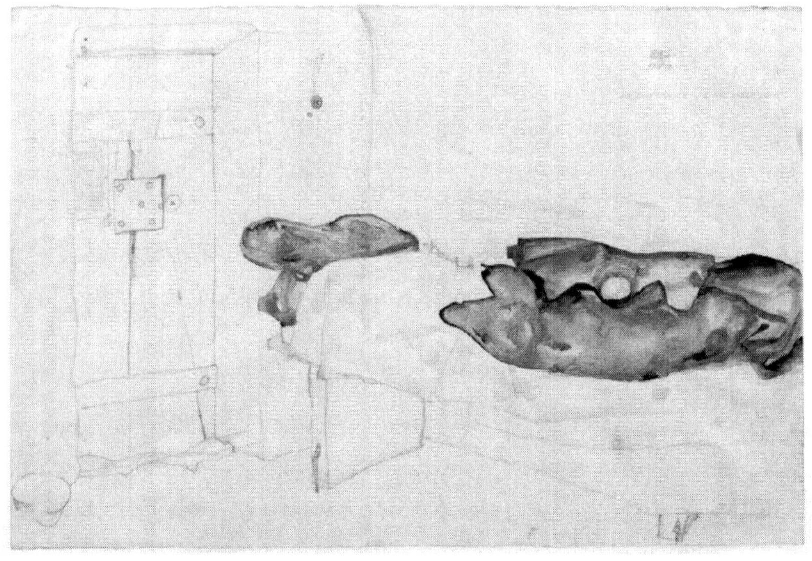

The Single Orange Was the Only Light

I listen close to the mumble of the town outside my walls. I have no window and on each wall is a thick plaster which deadens even my sounds to me so I listen close to the town mumble and I can tell what time it could be outside. And some bowl is brought to me passed through the door inside the door a bowl of food at best and the hand who brings this bowl to me is also another clock to use against the drawn-out day. But it is the quiet who so in the absence it holds can deeply enfuck the day and my hinge seems close to becoming rent.

Shaken shook loose I gather what was broughten me, the paper and an orange. The dusk inside this room is a perfect hoax. So night is always in its about to, my time is spended to arrange the time but until now. I cannot bring myself to the orange and peel off its outside. I put the orange on my wool blanket on my cot against the unended dusk in here.

This is the stillest life and so a cot, the door in its deep jamb, the planken legs of the slab cot, a rag at the bottom of the door so to better get the sound outside, the bedding and the gray wool blanket on top of that, the orange Wally brought set on top of that blanket, the brightest what I have in here gone versus all quiet and all plaster walls come tell me who would not take in this sight and know the better truth of what a piece of light can end up as.

And then I've put a curve in the wall corner it could have gone up straight but wouldn't vaulted make it more tunneled so I slough days here in such weighing.

I Feel Not Punished But Cleansed

The day after I lead you from here my room to the corridor who leads away. The door inside my door is gone open and from out of this I see to bring you. In night there is an oil lamp and the quiet, because it is now meant and watched up with the hour and the dark is only pushed off by this one lamp.

Give me to study the draw. The brooms and mops and a longhandled duster for the high corners the cobwebs who as if thrown there with no help from any bug just begin to be there and thicken with dust and that is my skin. The washbuckets in night turned over to dry the washbasins turned over to dry. Four rooms down the corridor's right wall for rooms like mine for a man like myself.

They have not all left me much as I have been removed from them my love my loves I am left to render corridors and brooms without you.

The bodies of the few I see here in this gaol have no burn. I could refuse to see the flame in it but rather how could a body who lives to lock another man into a room have any piece of fire in him but I do go and listen for it.

The Door to the Open

I still-life us to this.

Whatever is unchanged I will bring you with me to the next. And so I bring with me my unwoken self. Last night I left you with the lantern who sheds us in night with an only guide you were there with me I know that.

Unfolded unfolding to you is all what's left. My paper you brought I've wanted to fill in but find an outer line is enough to close in the color of where I live. My room I cannot leave I've been put here for a man who fucks his nearest it is no wonder we have only ourselves to consult at the ends of each strung-out day where the dusk clouds jumble up and we try to make sense of the shapes they've assembled.

Dearest man of my caption. I am straight I am unwandered I've back to you. No I am with you. To where we were. The door out to the open.

The Door to the Open

One of the latches is a simple hook and in the years of it spinning on the painted door has left a perfect circle etched around. There is a more formal deadbolt with a heavy black faceplate. At the top of the door is an iron grate for the wind to get through when the storm door is open on the far side of where I am. And farther still is a tree out there and some sparrows are there and I behold their movement from one branch to another branch as if this choosing were a deeply set rhythm of an animal a habit builded of a life inside the air with air moving throughout a day and managing between the gusts to land on one this branch who itself moves along with the moving air and the sun leans into them out there each sparrow angled slightly off against the next sparrow so that how we see the feathers laid in rows and layers each sparrow comes to us with a unique view for what I see of them is them small and in a dance among them to arrange themselves on branches each chooses I can now only guess at why each bird does happen to where I can only guess at when the storm door is open I can guess upon the motion of the door to the open which causes the hook to swing around spin into the painted wood and etch its circle there for this door to the outside is as far as I have known so far always closed.

If I knew more about the path of our moon I could plan it when the moon would itself be outside and visible from here through the iron grate at the top of the door to the outside. If I could mark the passing of the moon as notches in the handles of my tools or as a map of shadows on the floor of my shut room or as an arrangement of boulders set out in some perfect align with a leadstone for marking where the moon is according to the days if there was a window for me if there was a piece of night who got in through any break in the walls any split in the plenum of what's been built for a man like myself any seam who could open without some rule applied against it and allow in in night a speck of our moon so that I might apply a gauge to her to map when she will return like birds who come back according to some plan I'm unknown to. Her setted walk. Her blue path and my seas listen.

Two of My Handkerchiefs

Inside the gaol I have no mirror and I have no body to witness onto paper so leave to me this. A chair and what I have they have not yet from me removed. Handkerchiefs I use in daubing and to.

I give myself this true license. I sit on my dull bunk and court is had here a chair in drape of these two. My congress. With the only unneeded thing they left in here with me, my bunk I require if the limits of comfort extend to that and a stove and some blanket and bedding left here I wrap up in but the chair it serves almost no thing and no one but to almost taunt me with the idea that another is here with me or that another could be here with me. Or that I might move the chair to some spot for solace. Or there might be a view I could wage from the chair if it was set somewhere in particular but there is no view there is no vantage from anywhere in here there is only the blurred spokes inside me which I just spit out for thee.

This chair. Set out in front of me. She is what I set my kerchiefs on and stares me down. My bunk is best a seat as I've said in no direct ways and so I sit here against the other side of my room and she sits with her body bold and still to ask me what I'll do about her. You then be there and I'll assess thee. Your back set back at an angle so to enprouden you, your lap a flat invite set on our shared horizon, the sky of us will you please to please the room around you, I've left it blank for you. I'd rush to you I'd rush over but we've come to our fucked terms.

I'm a dog sleeping by you. Or you are the sleeping dog. Pads cupped in time with the breathing. Some far-off threat. Eyes hidden by the fur lids in tremble at the stage we set. Our dream home. The home we build in dreaming. What rooms our heads come up with. What rooms.

My island is a cot a bunk the bedding rough unplanned bedding though could I not compare my unplan to what they remain for me?

She, the chair. Accrue the sitting as she does. In two-point drawn, reducing down to the nil. Be still and I hang my green tights on you over your stiff back, over your proudness. And laid soft into your lap are kerchiefs laid soft and quiet your white seat is what I come to undo.

No room no corners of where no edge to hove or catch onto. I'll set you apart to lay bare the single what. So your proudness could equate in me the need to single out what you stand in for, your legs a strict setting, your back an upright gesture called to speak on what a good rule has limits to. I wait here on my bunk to hear what you could say to this idea of limits and the farness you could take this all.

Sitted here and asking you to move forward into the space between us. Could there be a different query?

Let us gather on my bunk in applaud of our one good chair. Let us thank who was it did the kindness to leave her with us. Let us praise us our lord for the kindest the smallest kind gestures we have for those we cage in to the smallest cells.

Let us clean us.

And let us acknowledge the greater sum of our days. The crossing of the sun and moon. The stars who if we fell into the deepest well we'd see in the middle of our day in their wide arcs.

Organic Movement of Chair and Pitcher

I've seen the sea and I know what the clouds do when they come down to the sea.

And I've small-towned it in between. The laden land. Who I stretch to come into grips with. Believing what I need and then what I come to.

My sand is an island I've already said. Turned on her side so we are here: the sided chair believe me I come to view only as a stranger; what you've become; what we've lost. My cities of what lost come back to speak clearly this dear aside. Let me unwander. Present us with the some. Dear jug, who's been lefted with a chair in uselessness, my jug lefted, left here to remind us all we've emptied our lot and need refill, the brimming up of us into the next.

Why would I not tip upon its side the chair left here for me as the only thing here to contemplate the missingness of some other why would I not upend it and leave it as a message to them as a message to me I don't require you I am full without you I am entirely without thee I tip thee as such. The jug has another purpose wholly of a job I now have water and before I had none and my day is now on water days noted. But the chair in this room could only serve so many uses or many uses one of which is that it is another who denotes a space inside the space I have another is the fact a bald fact who grows in time in baddish time the fact that I am alone and truly so it is the very point and my alone is then set up against an empty chair so that I may consider it as a vessel and consider it as a limit for my own setting and I may consider who might come to be upon it and when and at what angle and with eyes upon me in what way and legs positioned in what aparts and the tilted ends of our mouths do say as much as an entire room of eyes who would it be here in this room with such a mouth and corner of the mouth so the chair elicits from me the very question for if the chair was not here with me there would be no reason to have to wonder at it.

Organic Movement of Chair and Pitcher

I come to you and balance you there on your edge and let you fall over I let you fall over. Now sit and let me hold thee. Drawn with my jug. The memento. One last I please.

Art Cannot Be Modern. Art Is Primordially Eternal.

Surrogate? Kerchief or stockings. Neither cast a full glance upon this. Collect the guesses and chuck them in the sea and gather: it's a garment though no wide reason should fall upon this same blue twist or shirts laid over the chairback.

The stove up on its plinth. Crude base we stance you on. Who lifted you? A man in charge or other? Let's up to the plinth or that risen floor there.

I'll set the blue fabric on a chairback for the first sketch. I bring it to me and keep it close enough to scent for the second, there's not a smell enough I come to this as such its depth I'll draw it in as much as I can get it is what'll bring me back to the room of my Wally the land of the breathing the rooms of more exits set out for the living.

Face the chair away from me. That is a choose I can make in this. What I don't even need can be told as such. What I don't require for me to sit in peace can be told in how I turn the chair away from me so that each no one who sits I needn't even address I am enough for me at times I am enough today for me.

And I'll add a chair to double what I fucking don't require in this. I've room to put you here and facing away as well. Also turned from me I'll see your back and depict that for that is all I could need today so full and I'm enough.

Hindering the Artist Is a Crime, It Is Murdering Life in the Bud

I've cruxed you fuckers. Peaked out I've run a course and on a steep downside I find my today is wholly cut in two and each half fucked off to the side.

They've unbrought any food today. It was an answer to my yesterday standing up well. It's not as if I know how long I'll be here and so I guess I make a guess and today I get dragged down.

With no mirror I gut myself to pretend who's up above me. I couldn't look down upon myself without gods to hold me there. There could be no argument there I go ahead to gather. But yet I'm up above me and I'm needing a meal and a whole piece of sleep with full dreams in it I could use as well and without these I go floated up above I call to those engrounded and ask why I am chosen to rise here I have risen to be above me and I see down my gauntness is a second thought my wrap is the first and it is red. An outer line of my wrap is like an island drawn on some map fucked out of the lost stacks of true maps and most of which lie shambling in fate's eddies corners hove up in charts linted up to drift there no other way could they all land. An outer line around the red and around the gray woolen blanket who keeps my feet warm and some yellow I could only know inside the when.

I'm up above me. I've been lifted here and from the recall I have of me I sketch a crude and thinned cheek and I garner an extra space between the eye and its eyebrow as if I am open to any suggest. And as I might so be. I've no hands or legs or any limb. My island is drawn so that I might upon it with only my gaze depict in structured deeds I call upon I depict instead upon this perspectiveless cot drawn and I'm in red and I look back to you for once.

I'm unshaven. My hair has been reduced and I could ask for why they shear a man who sits alone. Is it to set us all in the same undifferent cell?

I sketch me from guesses, how my eyes would look from up here on how they feel, sockets gray and shaded my eyelids weighted down but I look down upon me and I am there in my red wrap.

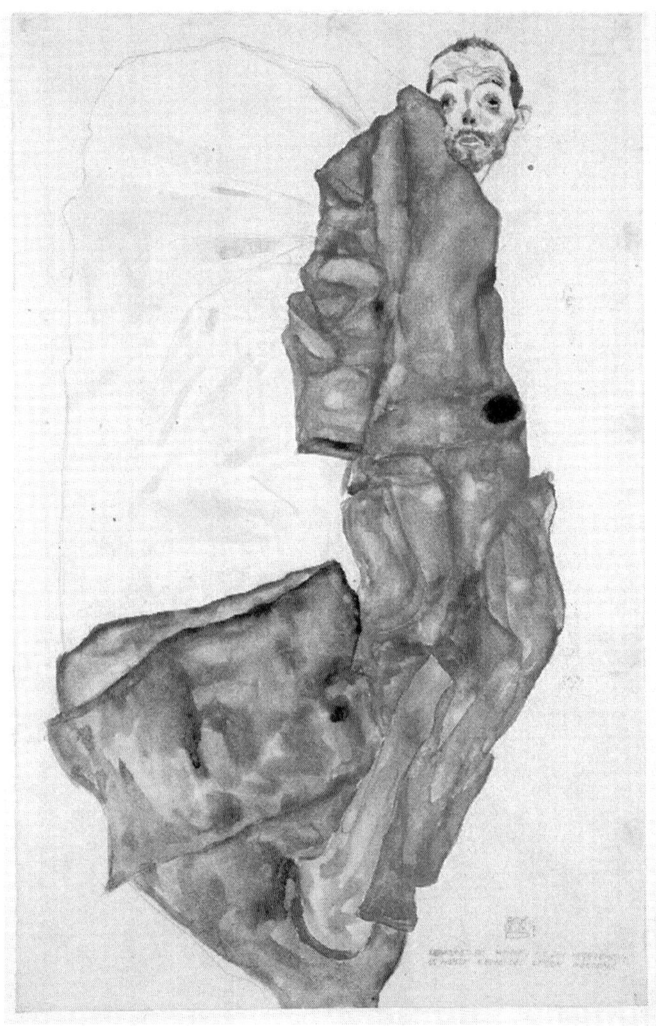

Prisoner

On my cot sitting I pour out a puddle from my jug. I pour and add to it and it becomes a looking glass enough so that I see my face at last. I am unsure if I've seen me like this, or unwilling to be sure. My cupped eyes and my dark beard and the hair they've brought away from me. I might not look at me head on. I'll corner my eye at me.

I am interested in you. Who have become this man I see in a puddle between my feet. Who rounded you up I'm beyond but who now looks as you do and the path inside this room who led you to this. What days have been who drag you through to now. The look you look back to me with how this is at all a possible look. But look I cannot help but submit to this. I cannot look away.

Gray is gray. The woolen blanket has shades of what itself is folded and tucked and ridged under. I'll mote the darker shades and burn off the silvers nearest me. My wrap before I'm wrapped up in it. Laid there crumpled as if I were within it. Leaving at the top a hollow where I'll lay my head. Turned sideways but until then my wrap I'll color in please. The grays I spread out on what I've made a pallet of, the black wiped across it to give me the full spectrum of blacks and grays and through to no color but I apply it as if it were as such.

The hollow I've left I pronounce my sunken head and my eyes. Turned on a side I corner me to you.

For Art and for My Loved Ones I Will Gladly Endure to the End

The child who balls himself up it is a done child or he is a child given over to capture. I pull the woolen blanket clawed down on me I have a spindle finger claw who drags a blanket tight down on me.

I'll turn the other hand to itself a claw down upon my cot. My rough sheets I sleep in. The possible endlessness of what this room decides for me. The clawn sheets I must. The clawn down on me woolen blanket I see the creases I've made on me pulled down over the balled-up child.

I'll again leave a hollow. As if I only had the charcoal and the russet shades I build a body into me. My blanket's terrain fleshed, it is my hands I build with the reddish shade, my cheeks flush and my ears but it is my captive mouth I duly color in the most russet the reddest the first stroke of the red I've made I lay it down there and my lips come to the color. My wrist my handback. My fingers the first time I see us here with hands is it true I've gone until now, though I see my hands and each is drawn in its gaunt spindle the clawed hand I'm left with you.

My Wandering Path Leads Over Abysses

I've unfolded a new wrap. Created three new oranges for us. The tapestry an olden theme I come to recall for us as the smell of an aunt's parlor recalls the events there. If we last here together please don't believe I've done nothing for you.

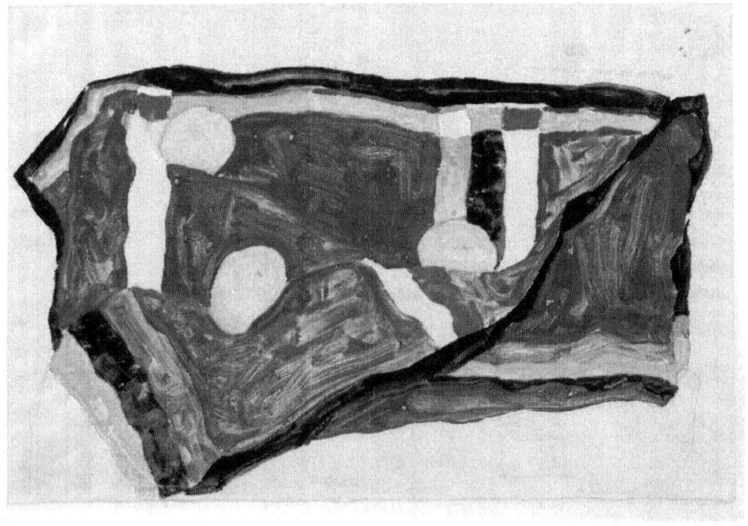

THE HISTORY OF OXFORD, MASSACHUSETTS

HOW WE MEND US

There's an older story in my family that goes like this. The story says my grandmother put her children in a foster home when they were five and six or so. My mother and my uncle. So she could live her life. Her husband, my grandfather, had left her for another woman. Josephine.

My mother doesn't carry with her any resentment over this. At least none that she mentions aloud. Her brother, my uncle, never forgave his mother for this.

I have inherited my mother's ability to forgive. Or to not remember, which is not the same as forgiving. The difference is what we carry in the body. I have inherited my mother's ability to trust the good intentions of others. So she could live her life.

There is a photograph of my grandmother. She's in her mid-twenties maybe, standing on the roof of a building in Manhattan or Brooklyn. She's dressed like a flapper with one of those thin bellish hats who hug the skull. With fringe.

She footnoted her collected Shakespeare and left her own table of contents at the front. Her cherished lines. Soliloquies and sonnets. I could learn enough from this table as any. I inherited this book when my grandmother died. Or at least it was given to me then. I left the collected Shakespeare at my mother's house, among my grandmother's books, because it had always been there.

There's another photograph of my grandmother. She's sitting on a couch with sisters, brothers on the floor in front, an apartment in Brooklyn or Manhattan, uncle someone to me, Great Uncle Stan or Uncle Bob, not smiling and an uncle's face when it goes dark is darker for the uncle in it, that Great Uncle Stan gaze. Easy enough to take a lamp and make a thing of it. The rug. The window shades. Stan's white shirt I don't even know if I have a great uncle who went by the name of Stan.

I remember an Uncle Bob, some Duncans, a house on Cape Cod where the water from the rising tide ran up near where they lived and filled in the channels of a salt marsh and I was there when I was three or so. There were cousins and these cousins looked like ducks.

I never thought homely, something near the home, or of the home, should be unfortunate.

How my grandmother on my mother's side lived was unallowed but she went ahead. How much of your life is your own she might have said inside, and how much of it is rote?

I asked my mother about my grandfather. Her father. Lincoln.

We got to when the skiers how the skiers found his body
on the hill behind his house in Fitchburg.
We got to when he didn't want his children
to be raised by strangers.
We got to Lincoln who never sold car parts
he sold Campbell's soup my grandfather on my mother's side.

My mother was born in Worcester, Mass, the daughter of a salesman of Campbell's soup and a woman of Scottish descent. A woman—tall, intelligent, stubborn, Scottish, Duncan, hard-headed, sure of what she was.

We got to Lincoln, to his home in Fitchburg, to his second wife Josephine, to his job at Independent Lock Company, to the ILCO stamp on padlocks and keys.

The footnotes gather my grandfather, Lincoln. His hairline is mine now, they say. He handed down his voice to me my mother tells me when I say a thing loudly, unchecked. His ghost in how I speak comes into the room his ghost only noticed by my mother.

We witness what's inside the day when we're young. To witness is the first act of unfolding. To play a part is the next. To have it all come visited down upon you firsthand and no other possible hand is when the body begins to keep a tab. These olden receipts are the work of us. Blown off a desk and under shut doors, left in laundered pockets, bookmarked and most often hidden though our own best self wouldn't cop to it.

My mother wasn't raised by strangers though Lincoln made the case.

It's as if we lay the underpinning and hang it up for reference.

What I say is what I know of it. Lincoln made the case his daughter and his son were being raised by strangers. I don't know why he said this or even if he did. I don't know if it was heard. He had a second wife by then. His first wife, the mother of his children, my grandmother, was in no state to take him back, I'm told. Not long after this he went behind his house in Fitchburg and went up the hill. This was in the winter.

Witness the boarding house. My grandmother lives there alone. Her children are in a foster home. Her husband off with Josephine for years. Her children visit her at the boarding house in Worcester on odd weekends. It is in the winter. Witness the young, her daughter and son, my mother and uncle, witness these young at the small dinner table when the common phone rings at the boarding house and my grandmother goes out into the hall and then comes back and witness how she sits down at the table with her children. Witness how her stare is off and far away and then witness what it is she tells her children.

We keep a tab for this and we keep a tab for what strangers did to us and we keep a tab hollowed in us for what else needs its away.

We learn to be kind too late.
Truly kind.
To guard another's happiness.
Truly kind.
Though truly this could be my own receipt.

THE BOOK OF MARK

Esther never mentions God.

The Book of Micah includes this simile: *Like waters poured down a steep place.*

The Book of Lamentations of Jeremiah ends with a question: *Art thou exceedingly angry with us?*

Mark is the second book of the New Testament, written before the fall of Jerusalem in AD 70. The Book of Mark was a source for the books of Matthew and Luke. The other source for the books of Matthew and Luke is Q. The German word for source is *quelle*. Q does not exist, but it can be guessed. Matthew + Luke = Mark + Q. Solve for Q.

A bible on the bottom shelf of a bookcase in the room where I write. Between two books on the American Civil War.

In the first chapter of Mark, we learn that Jesus was baptized by John and Jesus healed the sick, among them a leper who was instantly cured by the touch of the hand of Jesus.

A faith healer my father brought me to when I was nine. An outdoor shrine we stood in the sun as far back. An audience on a hill. I might have been on my father's shoulders. The faith healer was a father. Diorio. A priest who stunned the sick and broken with his hand. He was small from where we stood. He knew the numbers of his broken. Will the six who are with us today with arthritis of the knees come forward and approach the stage. And they did. Stooped. Shuffled. Carried. Stiff.

The father laid a hand on each and each was thrown backward by some wind or shock who visited. I wasn't called up. My father wasn't cured. We waited far back with our hidden ills and left early.

In Mark, Jesus withdrew with his disciples to the sea. Because there were so many followers and so many sick, Jesus told his disciples to get a boat ready in case the crowd became unruly and dangerous. The son of God asked his disciples to ready a boat.

Mark was my father's best friend. Mark Sanella. My father and Mark listened to jazz and smoked cigarettes and drank beer and talked into late nights a jazz around them on the record. The basement at Ball Street or driving in night in Oxford, Mass.

There are no books or maps I can trace back to this.

In Mark, Jesus gets a boat ready. Also in Mark, four associates of a paralytic removed the roof of the room where Jesus was preaching and lowered down into the room the paralytic on a pallet. In Mark, Jesus controlled the weather and the roughness of the sea, sent two thousand pigs to their death by drowning, split a loaf of bread between five thousand men, walked on the surface of the sea to the astonish of his disciples, and restored the hearing and the speech of a man who lacked both.

Just after feeding four thousand followers with seven loaves of bread and a few small fish, Jesus smartly got into his boat and left with his disciples.

In Mark, there's talk of the saltness of salt and the salt of fire, or the fire of salt, and the suggestion to salt yourself and be at peace with one another.

The blind have their blindness removed and the first things they see are trees in motion but they later learn those trees are men.

One night my father and Mark ran out of gas and Mark ran miles along the shoulders of the black roads to the service station and then ran back to the car with a jerry can where my father was waiting. Mark was an athlete. Track and field. Or maybe it wasn't a service station but Mark's house and back. Or early morning. Or raining. Cross country.

A light rain.

There are no maps I can trace back to this. No books to look it up in. What I make of my recollection is a faded rag and left somewhere to settle.

I don't know what my father knows.

Of land I'll inherit an acre of it that has a stone wall on the west, south and east lot lines. I hid things in the west wall when I was young when the wall was over my head and milkweeds taller than me grew in the field downhill behind it. This lot has been for sale for years but no one has made an offer. The sign by now it must be gone or faded.

Peter, in Mark, under the spell of the vision of a shimmering Christ, sees also visions of Elijah and Moses. Peter offers to build a booth for each of his visions.

In the Book of Mark, my father and Kenny Berthiaume have a plan to meet Mark at a rendezvous spot after Mark sets fire to a vacant house. My father and Kenny drove by the spot a few times but as the house became more involved and Mark didn't show, they drove home. Mark jogged the few miles back to Kenny's. It was July 4. One of their friends was a volunteer fireman and earned fifty dollars each time he was called to fight a fire. The plan was to split the money or to buy beer with some of it. Split the rest.

In the Book of Mark, Kenny Berthiaume's father was a pharmacist. A druggist. It was Kenny's father who put together the ergot formula for Mark's girlfriend to terminate what they came up with. Who was then inside her. The son of Mark, ended by the druggist. There would be no son of Mark.

As there is no Book of Mark.

There is no Mark at all. A cancer lived inside his brain. He returned to Webster Square after Miami and the Fontainbleau after UMass and the degree in hotel management after the tumor in his brain was found when he was seventeen.

He died at thirty-four, his Jesus year, the year he went inside a bed in Webster Square and his body waited with him until the end of them both.

I won't ask my father about Mark Sanella any longer.

In the Book of Mark, my father visits Mark at his bed in Webster Square. There is cancer in Mark's brain and there is a bed and there are some days left. But that is not the Book of Mark there is no Book of Mark.

In the Book of Mark, my father and Mark and Kenny are going to Webster Lake to borrow someone's motorboat. Mark's mother, a teacher in Oxford, is worried for her son's safety. After she's reassured that they'll be fine, and they won't be drinking, and the boat is a new ChrisCraft, Mark's mother is left without anything to say or worry about and as the boys are leaving she says at the last moment before they're gone, "Watch out for the propeller."

It was a house where no one lived so Mark with tinder and a match set fire to it. A rag and gasoline or a box of old news and a match in it.

On that night on July 4, Mark walked around the house the weeds up to his belt the night up above him. From where he was he could hear the cars pass on the state road a mile off and could hear if a car was coming up the dirt drive to this vacant house. The sounds in night more close than in the day.

The weeds up to his belt he went out through a near field and to a path who led to dirt side roads and the rendezvous spot the house behind him not yet bright but a fire in it began and Mark stepped high and began to walk faster away from the house he lit.

No one came to meet him at the rendezvous spot. He waited and the house across the couple fields burned well and firemen arrived to mostly watch the vacant house go up and then go down. He waited in a field a couple fields away and his ride was missing so Mark continued through the fields and weeds in parallel to the state road and walked himself the five or so miles back to his home.

They found a tumor in him. He'd been prodded for years. Tested. Drawn. Injected. Held. Shot. Written up. Diagnosed. Biopsied. Re-tested. Assured and then leveled with. Drawn. Waited. Drawn. Kept for observation. Tested. Monitored. His returns were booked.

Died his Jesus year. Half ago at seventeen they found the tumor after headaches and his vision went awry.

Mark was in Miami and walked the halls of the Fontainbleau.

He never married.

I don't know if he smoked and there is no Book of Mark.

There is proof we never lose touch with one another.

I fell in a frozen stream when I was eight. A stream down past that acre lot.

My grade-school friend Mike Martel was left-handed.

This is true. You can check. You can look it up.

Of habits I'll inherit the attic habits my father wore and his before him. Inherited mannerisms of the heart. Handing down some need for home and how gin sheds a day and there are few words to note the weather of the heart.

The second paragraph of a biography is also an obituary.

He was melancholy and introverted though easily amused.

Or not *though*. Therefore.

Mark's father Frank was the superintendent of schools in Oxford, Mass, and his mother Helen was a grade-school teacher. Watch out for the propeller. Mark's sister Lee was sapphic and moved to California. When Mark was seventeen a tumor was discovered in his brain. This would have been around the year 1952.

I don't know how brain tumors were treated in 1952. I could look this up. Mark lived for seventeen more years, dying at the age of thirty-four in a hospice home off Webster Square in Worcester, the tumor in him took over and took him out.

After Jesus healed or restored he sometimes asked that his miracle be kept a secret. Keep this under your hat was his request, but they never did. Those who were healed never obeyed the Christ. "And he charged them to tell no one; but the more he charged them, the more zealously they proclaimed it."

I was a year old when Mark Sanella died. My mother, father and two sisters and me lived in Stamford, Connecticut. My father did not go to church with us on Sundays. He stayed home instead and worked on the New York Times Sunday crossword puzzle while the rest of the family went to Greenwich Baptist Church.

Mark graduated from UMass Amherst with a degree in hotel management and moved to Miami, Florida, to take a job at the Fontainbleau Hotel on Miami Beach.

I think one night my father told me he didn't go to church with us because he couldn't worship a God who would take Mark away from him. I don't know one night if my father ever told me this. There are some things you remember that never happened.

In Mark, Jesus dies. Jesus also dies in the books of Matthew and Luke. Jesus might die in Q but it's not likely. It's agreed the book of Q is a collection of things Jesus said. There's a term for this, for a collection of things Jesus said, but I can't remember what that is.

We celebrate Salome on the Sunday of the Myrrhbearers. It was Salome who went to the market for spices to anoint the corpse of Jesus in his tomb. When Salome arrived at the tomb the huge stone at the entrance had already been rolled away. Inside the tomb was a young man, sitting on the right side, wearing a white robe. Salome was sainted but this young man and his white robe it isn't known just what became of him. In passing he remains a footnote in the Book of Mark.

I was forty-nine when I wrote this. My father is alive and my mother is alive and my sisters are both alive. Mark is dead. Lee moved to California. Mike Martel was left-handed. You can look this up. You can look all of this up. We never lose touch with one another. This losing touch is not possible either in the footnotes, the margins, or along the wide trunk of the story.

THE HISTORY OF EARTH

Looking back as upon the stretches of tiles who in surface become our maps the ones skipped our lost or never laid ashlar. Filling in these pauses with the measurements of others—books nearby and raw footage of space and seas and some of it untrue. The place our unquiet eye leads us. Or bored or somehow unsated we take a few slow steps and decide to learn about geologic time and how the moon came to be.

On geologic time there were the periods of heavy bombardment. Millions of asteroids and debris impacting Earth which at the time had not yet cooled and was itself a ball of molten minerals. There is also the giant impact hypothesis. Something planetish the size of Mars hits Earth head-on. Some believe there was an ocean of magma. What would become the moon spun off from this collision and became debris that orbited Earth and over centuries coalesced. There is today no consensus on the details.

On extinction events apart from what this season visits us we sift a full catalog. Permian-Triassic or the Great Dying brought about it's possible in solo or in a clutch of pulses some drawn in oceanic methane yet some hold to account the Siberian Traps. Eighty-three percent of all genera extinct and this was the end of the Paleozoic Era. Two hundred million years later an asteroid eight miles wide impacted Earth near what is now the Yucatan and this is the theory of Alvarez. Almost eighty percent of all plant and animal life erased. The Mesozoic Era came to an end and teleost fish with it, so many of them sequential hermaphrodites.

The giant sloth and the camels of America. Giant armadillos weighing two tons each and American horses, mammoths, oversized cave lions and rodents the size of bears. The giant sloth reaching a height of twenty feet and weighing eight tons. These all exterminated over the course of about a thousand years after evolving and thriving on the continents of the present-day Americas for thirty million years.

Crossing from Siberia to Alaska and south past melting glaciers into North and then South America. The Holocene. An interglacial period of the Cenozoic. This is the original migration of humans from Africa to Asia to North America. Making many of ourselves. Moving on to settle in continual moving. Gathering and killing what was nearby until that too was gone. Continuing east to the wetlands of Alabama and south to the deserts of Central and South America, the jungles of Central and South America. Here in our blink.

Over the course of fifty million years of mutation and selection brought about the horse. The horse was then killed off in one millennia. On the arrival of humans, *Homo sapien*. On this the fossil record is not ambiguous.

Columbus and his boats who on false math augured into an unknown continent. He called them Indians even so and so began the first of four exterminations of the inhabitants of North and South America. Violence and disease against which there was no natural immunity.

India, once an island continent, moving inches a year toward Asia and causing on its arrival the upheaval of the Himalayas.

~ ~ ~ ~ ~

Two hours of an afternoon on the front porch. There is a breeze. Three tall sycamore trees near the house and growing through the railing of the porch is a honeysuckle vine and climbing up the front porch column is a Cecile Brunner rose bush that has started to bud. On each new rosebud are twelve or twenty aphids about the same shade of light green as the buds. The blind dog this afternoon moves from one spot of sun to a spot of shade and back again every ten minutes or so. There is often an afternoon breeze here. The wind chimes at the far end of the porch are almost too loud this afternoon. Three birds are on the lawn eating dandelion seeds. Four birds, sparrows maybe.

~~~~~

Australia, unconnected to any other continent, left to its own millions of years of disparate evolution. Megafauna, unlike any other on the planet, killed off to not return coinciding with the arrival of Asiatic *Homo sapien*. And so the *Homo sapien*—a sentient plague, a cloud, the summary of five hundred million years of vertebrate radiation.

The measurements of others. Two hundred and forty thousand miles from Earth to the moon. At an average speed of ten thousand miles an hour a ship can arrive in about twenty-four hours. Three men. Weightless. Hours earlier on land in Florida.

After any period of even general research into the history of mankind it becomes clear that our Earth is under no pact to let us in on why we exist at all.

~~~~~

There was a time when time began more recently. Before the Enlightenment, when sacred time led us to believe the beginning of our history was in the Garden of Eden. This was later revised to Armenia, where it was believed Noah and his boat came to rest after the flood. And floods were understood to be the cataclysmic events that marked the primary epochs of human history. If there was a flood and this flood killed off all mankind, including any written record of their existence, then this new postdiluvian world must be the true origin of civilization.

There was a time when it was believed the Earth was about six thousand years old. Calculations were made by biblical scholars who looked deeply into the passages of the Old Testament to determine how many years had passed since the creation of the Earth.

It was not until the Enlightenment when it was proposed that the Earth was much older than previously imagined. Based on calculations of the cooling of molten metals, Kelvin proposed that Earth was roughly a hundred million years old. This number also lent credence to the theories of Darwin and Lamarck, giving the once unfathomable spans of time required by these theories the millions of years to play out.

~~~~~

In fifth grade, when I was ten years old, for extra credit I baked a mixture of flour and water in the oven after putting it into a baking tray and pressing grooves in it with my finger. When it was cooked I painted in those grooves with blue paint to look like irrigation canals and next to those irrigation canals I painted green lines to indicate the food crops nourished by the water diverted there. This was the cradle of civilization. Sumer. Mesopotamia. The Fertile Crescent. Between the Tigris and Euphrates rivers. Where civilization began, or so.

There was no mention of Africa or how at all humanity appeared in Sumer. Looking back it seems even then, when I was ten, there was a kind of sacred or mystical quality to the cradle of civilization. Echoes of bible study must have filled in the cracks for what was missing in the narrative I received. But none of us ever mentioned that out loud and our teachers never said as much.

Men with robes, camels, walking across vast landscapes of sand
~~~~~

and dunes. This must be where the bible left off and where our school books picked up the story. In Sumer, with men pressing small shapes into clay tablets and diverting water from rivers off to where the crops were grown. It is believed, from the results of the most sophisticated scientific methods of dating potsherds and human remains, that Sumer was first settled about seven thousand years ago. This cradle of civilization.

~~~~~

The parietal art inside the Grotte Chauvet is estimated to be about thirty thousand years old.

Shark teeth and ancient mollusks and trilobites have been discovered on mountaintops.

Potsherds. Lithics. Debitage. What these are are gussied-up words for garbage.

Coprolite is the word for prehistoric turd.

There is a reason why middens are so important. The archeologist carefully brushes away the dirt to uncover one more piece of broken pottery, one more obsidian chip left behind from the building of an arrowhead, tiny bones of what was eaten, thousands of shells carefully separated and examined for clues on how they might have been used for something at all other than nothing and charcoal tells the story of what fuels cooked the flesh of what was run off cliffs to death. The bones of infants decorated by intricate costume jewelry and the crushed skulls of scoliotic elders. The story of a people and their deeds sung through the vibrant record of garbage. What's cast off defines us. What rots becomes our message. What remains after we've consumed all there is to consume within our practical reach, an unimaginable shelf of trash that sings the odd story of an everyday human. So we continue, gathering and casting off, gathering and holding on to an odd piece, our own shard or the cast-off flint who has an important shape, for
~~~~~

luck, a superstition, culling out the ordinary to give it meaning and to polish it, gathering and casting off, refining our jumble into the gem of that day, the stuff that assembled tells our chapter here or so we believe, and we bury our brightest stories for them only to be misread by the next.

ACKNOWLEDGMENTS

Thank you to Steven Gillis, Michelle Dotter, Chelsea Gibbons, and everyone at Dzanc Books.

Thank you to David McLendon and Jaclyn Gilbert for your careful and kind attention to early versions of this collection and for your invaluable input.

Thank you to Michael Krantz for the beautiful cover design.

I'd also like to thank the editors of the publications where some of these pieces were first published: David McLendon at *Unsaid*; Nic Leigh at *Territory*; David Winters and Andrew Latimer at *Egress*; Kasumi Borczyk at *Paraphase*; Andrew Gallix at *3:AM Magazine* and *We'll Never Have Paris.*

ABOUT THE AUTHOR

Russell Persson lives in Reno, Nevada. His first novel, *The Way of Florida*, was published in 2017 by Little Island Press, and was reprinted in 2025 by Baobab Press. His work has appeared in *The Quarterly, Unsaid Magazine, 3:AM Magazine, Egress, Paraphase Journal,* and other publications.